# PARADISE FIELD

# PARADISE FIELD
## A NOVEL IN STORIES

## PAMELA RYDER

TUSCALOOSA

FC2 is an imprint of the University of Alabama Press

Inquiries about reproducing material from this work should be addressed
to the University of Alabama Press

Book Design: Publications Unit, Department of English, Illinois State
Univeristy; Director: Steve Halle, Production Assistant: Jade Urban
Cover Design: Chris Lawrence and Pamela Ryder

Typefaces: Baskerville, Amamma Inline

Library of Congress Cataloging-in-Publication Data is available from the
Library of Congress
ISBN: 978-1-57366-063-1
E-ISBN: 978-1-57366-874-3

For Gordon Lish

# CONTENTS

Interment for Yard and Garden: A Practical Guide / 1

Paradise Field / 29

The Renoir Is Put Straight / 41

The Song Inside the Plate / 63

As Those Who Know the Dead Will Do / 67

Arrow Canyon / 83

Irregulars / 99

Somewhere in the North Atlantic / 105

Two Things / 113

Mitzvah / 115

Recognizable Constellations and Familiar Objects
    of the Night Sky in Early Spring / 139

Jerusalem / 153

Details of Grief / 177

Badly Raised and Talking with the Rabbi / 187

Inscription / 191

The Rhythm of Digging / 193

There's Nothing Here You'd Want / 195

In This Last Slipping-Past Year / 205

In Other Hemispheres / 213

Acknowledgments / 229

# INTERMENT FOR YARD AND GARDEN: A PRACTICAL GUIDE

### *Beit Olam* or a Home in the Earth

When a death is expected—as in the case of a family member, such as a parent—perhaps an elderly parent—or even more specifically, in the case of one's father, for example—decisions must be made as to the means of final disposition of the body. For the urban Jew, this usually constitutes burial in a cemetery outside the city limits, but those in suburban settings may consider interment in a yard or garden. To that end, a journeyman Soil Shifter can be had for hire. As he makes his rounds through the neighborhood, he is alerted to an impending death when the well-known "Death Angel" mushroom, *Amanita matzoa*, sprouts on the lawn of the dying. This particular species of *Amanita* is, of course, named for the Passover Angel of Death who delivered the Tenth Plague to Egypt, requiring the Israelites to bake unleavened bread and descend into the Sinai (although he was probably responsible for the rain of frogs, lice, and locusts as well). In addition, a Soil Shifter will stop at any house of the dead or dying where a *mitpachat* is displayed above the lintel or the deceased's *tallit* is hung

1

over the mailbox. If a *tallit* is used, be sure to cut off a corner fringe to signify that it will no longer be used as a prayer shawl, and that the deceased is no longer required to pray (not that a particular daughter recalled her father ever praying about anything, except when he said *Kaddish* at his own father's funeral, and that time he was audited by the IRS). And though the Soil Shifter will be readily available, it is considered an especially charitable *mitzvah* to forgo his services and, instead, dig the grave yourself. The deceased can offer neither reward nor gratitude for your labors, and because he cannot make his own *beit olam*, doing so for him is truly the final act of kindness. As it is written in Ruth 2:20: "Blessed be he who hath not left off his kindness to the living and to the dead."

The bereaved may have other, more personal motives in deciding to forgo the Soil Shifter and tackle the task himself. There may be old grudges and resentments regarding the dead, and amends that were never made. (If the deceased person was, for example, a father, then it is quite possible that the adult child, a daughter, for instance, may regret her actions during the father's illness and last days. She may not have heeded the assertion of Proverbs 17:22: "A glad heart is good medicine, but a broken spirit saps the strength of the sick." She would likely recall that her heart was hardly glad while caring for her father. She is likely to remember her impatience when he refused to eat, her revulsion when she scrubbed his dentures, her shame at holding his urinal or wiping his butt. She will recall the dietary restrictions she enforced to the point that there was little enjoyment left to him, i.e. "Lox? Forget it—too much salt." She may have been angry with the father, believing he could have "tried harder" to exercise, to take his heart medications on time, to get off his ass and walk with his walker and try to get his strength back, etc. She may lament her lack of expressions of endearment, believing that there would be the proverbial "more time" to resolve her ridiculous resentments regarding his apathy and absence during her childhood, especially now that she is well into middle age.) But there will be no atonement in these matters, of course—no forgiveness— and it is best that such a person simply attend to digging of the burial hole as *mitzvah* for its own sake.

Grieving individuals often require instruction in grave excavation. *Domestic Disposal of the Dead* (Vol. I & II), *Planning a Home Necropolis* (no longer in print), and *The History of Digging: Paleolithic Man to the Present* (Vol. I–IV) remain the classic texts, although they are often daunting to the bereaved. Many find it impossible to wade through lengthy discussions and instructions after the death of a family member or even as death draws near. This is especially the case when the accompanying compulsion "to be done with it" is a common reaction if the dying individual—a father, for example—had endured lengthy suffering and/or humiliation, i.e. bladder and bowel dysfunction (what a father might call "pissing and shitting myself"), tremor of the extremities (what he called "the shakes"), and advice/remedies suggested by well-meaning bedside visitors ("Gefilte fish? You want to kill him?"). And as Jewish law requires that the body be interred within twenty-four hours of death, perusal of a multivolume text is not possible. Therefore, the bereaved will find *Interment for Yard & Garden: A Practical Guide* to be both practical and comforting.

## Alternatives to Interment

The dead must be placed in the earth. This is Jewish law. G-d's directive to Adam was unequivocal: "You shall return to the earth, for you were taken out of it."—Genesis 3:19. And yet, non-observant, uneducated, or spiritually bereft Jews may consider other methods—namely Sky Burial, Carcass Conflagration, or Burial at Sea. Therefore, these alternatives warrant discussion here.

1—*Sky Burial* (in which the body is placed above ground for vulture consumption) was practiced by ancient Israelites during times of flight from persecution, when the process of digging through the rockbound desert soil would delay the escape of the living. Sky Burial remains in use today, but due to declining numbers of *Corvus corone* (i.e., Carrion Crow) species, there are fewer birds to feed on the body, and flesh removal is delayed. Sky Burial also brings with it the nuisance factor of birds (referred to as *Sky Schnorrers*) continuing to root and circle long after the corpse has been consumed. Observations of the lingering birds (*Schnorrer Sightings*) reveal that they retain an interest in familiar earthly events, croaking announcements in the voice of the newly departed/recently ingested person: "Candle-lighting at 6:23 tonight"—or voicing criticism regarding sights on the ground below: "This you call a *Sukkot* tent?" (In the case of a father, for example, whose bird might be circling in skies above the neighborhood at dusk, his remarks are likely to be more secular: "Who left all the goddamn lights on?")

2—*Carcass Conflagration* (with subsequent wind dispersion of char/ash) is clearly forbidden by Jewish law. This method is an especially abhorrent reminder of the extermination crematoria of just one generation ago. In addition to its obvious desecration of the body, reports of abnormalities in songbirds in the forests around Treblinka and Ravensbrück were well documented. Such deformities (avian caul, soot wing) have been so observed around present-day crematoria and are believed to be caused by tooth fillings which volatize during the intense heat of incineration and are spewed into the atmosphere as mercury vapor. (Not a factor, for example, in the case of a father who had no fillings—just badly neglected teeth, broken to the gumline under his dentures—as a result of a childhood fear of the family dentist and third cousin Morton Plotkin DDS, who smoked a cigar during dental procedures, was known to drop hot ash into the patient's lap, and gave a discount on extractions every Friday before *Shabbos*.) Despite the connotations, reduction of the body to char and ash is still regarded as a means of disposition by uninformed Jews or those influenced by the funereal practices of gentiles. In addition, the topic of carcass conflagration may be bantered about by simply irreverent persons (case in point: a dying father who—when asked about his wishes—was fond of saying, "Dead is dead" and "Who gives a crap?"—though near the end he reminded his adult daughter about the existence of a cemetery plot he "paid good money for" and in truth, had absolutely no inclinations toward a fiery end anyway). Nevertheless, even if the deceased had left instructions for conflagration, it is the obligation of those caring for the body to disregard such wishes and to provide a burial in accordance with the laws of the Torah.

Lastly, Carcass Conflagration can occasionally result in the troubling spectacle known as Ash Reorganization. During this phenomenon, airborne particles spewing from crematorium smokestacks rise, regroup, and hover in the shape of the deceased—sometimes for several days—before eventual dispersal (or when wind velocity exceeds thirty mph).

3—*Burial at Sea* is sometimes requested by individuals who are wistfully enamored of the ocean. They decide that upon their demise, their charred remains be dispersed (or what is more commonly referred to as "scattered") upon the waves from a scenic seaside overlook or the railing of a boat. This practice is clearly contrary to Jewish law. But what of the more complex problem that arises when a Jew happens to die at sea, as ships will not alter their course when a death occurs. Such a situation is not unusual during a cruise vacation, when the elderly (a sizable percentage of cruise passengers) are more likely to succumb to onboard hazards: the *chazeri* served at the twenty-four-hour, all-you-can-eat buffet; the diarrhea and subsequent dehydration caused by the aptly named "Bon Voyage Virus"; the falls that inevitably occur when old folks careen around in their cabins in rough seas; and the third-rate doctors cruise lines employ (which might be exactly the worries of an adult daughter, for instance, when her elderly father had been cajoled into a week-long "Epicurean Cruise of the Caribbean" by his big fat selfish so-called girlfriend and world-class *kvetcher* who never really gave a whit about him anyway, and was mainly interested in working her way through the aforementioned buffet and desert display at a pace fast enough to work up a good *schvits*). And although the daughter worried that the exertions of the trip—*schlepping* the luggage, the aforementioned *dreck* that cruise lines call food, the very real possibility that the to-and-fro motions of the moon-driven sea might cause the big girlfriend to roll over on her father while he slept and cause his suffocation, he made it back alive—thanks be to G-d he did. He made it back and nothing that bad happened, nothing really bad—although his favorite hat blew off his head by the brisk wind off the stern—the cap he was awarded that time he made a hole-in-one at the Del Ray Country Club on the sixth hole—which is a downhill 250-yard, par-three with a dogleg left—and he watched from the rail as the hat sailed up into the smokestack steam, briefly disappeared into the mist, reappeared again overhead, spun almost back to him on a starboard gust, was taken again by a spume of sea, and finally lost in the foam. If something bad had happened—really bad, G-d forbid—such as any of the things a father was prone to, including stroke, blood clot, burst aorta, or infarction of the heart—he would have been buried at sea. This would free the big woman to disembark at the next scheduled stop without the old man along, i.e., "without George slowing me down" (as she often remarked), and to suspend her grief for a duty-free stint of spending (perhaps another bracelet from the Cartier in Freeport, a few touristy *tchotchkes* as gifts, and it's always a good idea to pick up a dozen big bars of Swiss chocolate when you've got the chance). Deposition in the earth is not an option at sea, of course, unless the decision is made to delay earth burial and place the corpse in the ship's cold storage with the pork tenderloin, *khazer-fisl*, and assorted *treif* for what may be an extended period of time—clearly a desecration of the body. In such circumstances, Burial at Sea is preferable. There will be no grave-marker and no place of remembrance, but the deceased can rely upon G-d's mercy: "When you pass through the waters, I will be with you."—Isaiah 43:3. The shrouded body is simply placed upon a board. The board is set upon the rail and tilted seaward. The body slides away, slipping beneath the waves and into the foam like an old hat.

After notions about the alternative methods of corpse disposition are dismissed, and the choice is made to obey Jewish law, the bereaved must then decide: burial with or without a coffin. A Jew's coffin must be a simple wooden box, constructed without nails or metal hinges to ensure that it will—like the body—return to the earth in its entirety. However, burial without a coffin is certainly permissible, even recommended. Interment of the body wearing only a soft white shroud is an ancient Jewish practice that honors the dead, and the sight of an actual body in the burial hole helps awaken the living.

### Excavational Patterns

Shovel acquisition is the next task. According to a notation in the *Jewish Magical Papyri of the Second Temple Period*, the shovel used to dig a hole in which to place a body must not be a new one. Maimonides, in an apocryphal chapter of his *Guide for the Perplexed*, explains that a new shovel is "inauthentic" and cannot be utilized as a functional talisman. The digger therefore should obtain a shovel previously used for digging a burial hole—though use in any other type of excavation will do.

This is not a problem in more rural or country settings where hole digging is nearly habitual. In such areas, a peek in any barn, outbuilding, or shed, will reveal a variety of useful implements—half-moon hoes, soil scuffles, mulch scoopers, and of course, shovels. But when a death occurs in more suburban districts, cries of "Where can a shovel be had?" are common.

Suburban Jews rarely dig or engage in yard and garden maintenance (possibly a result of the ancient exodus from original agricultural exploits to urban occupations). And when they must, they are often exceedingly inept. (Case in point: an adult daughter may fondly recall the father's antics in attempting to mow the lawn: the cursing that ensued as he repeatedly ran the power mower over the electric cord, and the pathetic repair of the breaks with adhesive tape. Or the time he nearly amputated a finger with the hedge clippers.) However, during the relatively brief period between the vernal equinox and the summer solstice, physiological changes take over. A combination of photoperiodism and circadian rhythms trigger pituitary secretion of Digging Induction Substances, which, in turn, result in the three *Excavational Patterns*:

1—*Atavistic Agronomy*: The suburban homeowner is stimulated by agricultural tendencies that flourished before the displacement of the Jewish farmer: he decides to grow his own food. He falls prey to the color photographs and descriptions in seed catalogues, i.e. "Big Boy Carrots—crisp and colorful, perfect for a holiday *tzimmes*" and "Potato Mezzo Luna—truly tantalizing tubers for pancakes or *kugel*." He purchases seed, shovel, and spade. He tills the garden plot, mulches and composts, and carefully sows according to seed packet instructions. (Or, as in the case of a certain father, spreads a bag of topsoil on a sunny spot, tears the seed packets open with his teeth, and sprinkles seeds willy-nilly. He then soaks down the whole thing with the garden hose for the first and last time, relying on sporadic rainfall thereafter.)

While *Atavistic Agronomy* results in shovel acquisition and some degree of cultivation, it quickly becomes obvious that a vegetable garden requires tending: weeding, spraying, watering, pinching, fertilizing, thinning, mulching, composting, and pest removal. Sprouting plants are often consumed by local wildlife (rabbits, whistle pigs, and the like), crowded out by weeds, or killed off during dry spells. Eventually, the would-be gardener concedes defeat (or—for instance—a father realizes that his wife would never serve up fresh vegetables anyway, and would continue to do nothing more than open a can of Green Giant creamed corn).

2—*Denning*: The homeowner is driven to construct a subterranean shelter. This activity is prevalent in the autumn, but can occur in any season during an apocalyptic threat: a period of potential earth-meteor collision, nuclear winter, or infrastructure failure. The evolutionary mechanism for this activity is unclear, but is thought to be associated with primitive burrowing instincts before winter sets in. To construct his underground living quarters, the homeowner buys his shovel and begins to dig (or in the case of a particular father who does not actually *buy* a shovel because he has a brother-in-law in retail who knows a guy who can get one that "fell off a truck" which is cheaper than wholesale even).

Eventually, denning behaviors cease. The unforeseen expenses involved in construction of the subterranean shelter (septic field, sump, solar panels, thermonuclear protection, etc.) ultimately halt the project. (A father's comments typically include "Never throw good money after bad" or a simple "To hell with it.")

3—*Pseudo Veld Syndrome*: The suburban homeowner unconsciously yearns for the environs of his *Homo erectus* ancestors: the South African veld along the Limpopo River—a landscape of broad savannahs with a scattering of brush, and the open vistas that facilitate the sighting of game. The results of these longings can be seen around nearly every suburban home: yards that are essentially an expanse of grass (lawns) with carefully spaced plantings (shrubbery). To recreate this landscape, the homeowner purchases a rake, hoe, and shovel, and prepares his weedy property for reseeding by hacking up and turning over the old sod. He then purchases specimens of commonly planted shrubs—usually ornamentals such as *Arborvitae* and yew (*Taxus brevifolia*). These arrive by truck and require several men to unload them, due to their unwieldiness and the weight of their bulky root balls bound in burlap. Undaunted (at least initially), the homeowner rolls up his sleeves and begin to dig (or in the case of some fathers, for instance, head back inside the house for a shot of scotch before getting down to business).

The transformation of his property from ordinary yard to ancestral hunting environs predictably arouses blood sport instincts in the suburban male. He then typically conceals himself in the newly planted shrubbery with some sort of weapon at the ready (firearm, crossbow, spear, or steel-rimmed yarmulke), keeping an eye out for nonexistent antelope and kudu, but taking potshots at roaming cats or unleashed dogs. When this proves unsuccessful, he disregards the biblical assertion against killing ("G-d's mercies extend to all His creatures."—Psalms 145:9) and takes to the November woods to stalk wildlife with a group of other men—both Jew and Gentile—similarly affected. The white-tailed deer (*Odocoileus virginianus*) being plentiful in both rural and wilderness districts, is the object of the slaughter.

Certain words of incantation are spoken during these weekend expeditions: Cull. Doe. Buck. Bag. Rack. Points. Blade. Skin. Gut. They are repeated while motoring to what they refer to as "the mountains" or "upstate." They are uttered while settling into a lodge with a rustic décor (antler light fixtures) or an old motel (pine paneling) and again the evening before the hunt while gathering at a drinking establishment where dusty specimens of taxidermy gaze down upon them (the head of a glass-eyed deer, the snarling raccoon perched on a stump, the female bear posed with her cub). Come early morning, while the men are pulling on blaze orange or camouflage jackets and ear-flapped hats in the predawn dark, the words are spoken once again, silently at times, and once again on their walk though the woods as the day is breaking. They will follow the random marks in the snow and speculate on the size and direction of the prey. They will examine and discuss a "trail" of broken twigs and attempt to interpret its meaning. They will point their guns at every sound—the shh shh shh wing-beat work of crows passing over, the creak of wind-swinging tree—and they will peer down their gun sights at nothing. Success will have little to do with the accuracy of their aim or their ability to track or any skill at all—but instead, upon their readiness to shoot at anything that moves.

To be sure, some come home with a story of how a carcass came to be slung and tied across the car roof or lashed to the bumper, and the bloodiest of labors still ahead of them. Others return with only a coating of snow on the roof of the old Desoto or the Buick or the Pontiac sedan (a father, for instance, returning to a wife who had been hoping there would be nothing to chop and wrap and pack in the freezer. That father returning home to a child—let's say a daughter—yes, a daughter—why not?—who had waited out that November weekend as she had done each year after childhood year, upstairs in her room busying herself making a model of the solar system, or cracking geodes with a hammer ("What's going on up there?" shouts the mother) or re-reading *Three Little Foxes* or *Black Beauty* or *The Catcher in the Rye*. She rambles around the yard and frozen garden where last summer's weeds stand sparkling with frost. And after nightfall, the daughter lies awake in her bed in the early dark that winter evenings bring, waiting for the headlight lights to slide across her bedroom wall and the car door to slam the way the father slams it. And finally, to hear the father jiggle the key in the lock and the rough way he presses down the thumb latch and the way he kicks the door so that she knows—as soon as that, she knows. She hears the father come solidly up the stairs, and now the third step makes its terrible creak. She sees the shape of him and his earflap cap as he stops and stands at her bedroom door. Would he come in and find too many bears in her bed, or say she has a dolly one or two too many, and would he sweep them out of her arms and to the floor? Would he slam that shut, too, in the one-handed way he liked to slam it? The way that hard but good-looking man in the movie slammed it when the woman walked out and the boy ran away and the grandfather died because his cows were herded into the giant ditch and the men on the rim picked up their rifles and shot down into all the cows in the ditch, and when all the cows were dead or you could hear them dying, the men put down their rifles and pushed the big piles of earth and bulldozed them over—that was the way the father liked to slam it, even though he knew the daughter did not like to be shut up in the dark—she told him as much, once or twice or a hundred times but maybe he didn't remember, no he must not have remembered—time after time and year after childhood year, until the daughter—the child—hoped that once, just once he might come through the door saying, "Pamela!—how's my girl?" and smelling of pine-smoke and cold wool clothes, his rough face against her cheek, the father back home in a way he never was—at least not any time she remembered. Would he come home to tell his wife the story of the woods and the snow and the gun—in the way he once must have told her things— he must have, once—before she was born—the way they used to be in an old photograph? "Our honeymoon," the mother told the daughter—the coconut palms, her father's arm around her mother's waist, the water sliding up the sand in shapes of lace along their feet. And this time telling his wife and daughter, "Got one" or whatever it is a man, a hunter, a father telling a story of killing would call himself after he had done what he had set out to do. The daughter imagines him holding the head of it in his arms, the neck cut away at the shoulder, the fall of blood—a trail of it from the car and the ropes; a leakage of the lolling tongue from front door through the living room, dripping down even in her daytime dreams because gravity pulls everything down and keeps her in her seat at the supper table and keeps her in her bed so she won't float away when she sleeps, keeps the planets of the solar system in their places so they won't spin away and collide with the stars, keeps the birds flying between earth and sky where they won't whirl away all wild and willy-nilly. She sees how it must have been: the deer standing against the moon-blue snow with the last of the stars in the great smoke-like spill of a galaxy spinning above him, his mouth pulling on a bitter sprig of spicebush with his long deer snout. Dawn spreads over the snow so he does not see the shadows moving toward him until the gun is raised, and then comes the bursting of his body. Quail rise from their cover. Snow slides from an evergreen bough. It would be quick, she imagines. It must be so, and without the moans or movements that she has heard the dying make. No chase. The butchery, the beheading, with eyes still clear—brown and like her eyes would look if she were dead—but that part would not be trouble, that part of it would be all right, would just have to be all right, so that her father for once would have his day, his proud and good and happy day.)

*Pseudo-Veld Syndrome* will end of its own accord. As is the case with other *Excavational Patterns*, it is self-limiting. Enthusiasm will wane with a succession of unproductive hunts. And even for those who manage to bring home and consume a carcass, the inconveniences of the outings diminish the call of the veld. The expeditions become more infrequent. Eventually they are given up entirely.

### Shovel Revitalization

Shovels are abandoned when the excavational activities cease. Most are relegated to basements and garages (or in the case of a certain father, for instance, who left the shovel leaning against the side of the garage for the next fifty-seven years). It is often only after a future death—perhaps decades later—that they will be needed, and the quest for shovel acquisition begins once again.

In most cases, the forsaken shovel will be in a poor state of repair. The ferules at the handle or shaft will be loose. The blade edge will be dull, the scoop surface rusted, the rim-rest for the foot caked with soil. While it is tempting to ignore these imperfections and begin the digging, taking a few moments for repairs is well worth the trouble. Hose off any accumulations of caked-on soil. Use a screwdriver to tighten the ferule with a twist or two. Remove rusted areas on the scoop surface with a medium grade steel wool. And finally, use a file to sharpen the edge of the blade.

## Site Selection

Site selection, or "Where To Dig?" is the next task. Associates of the deceased will inevitably suggest a place under a tree—a picturesque setting that the corpse would approve of, as in, "He would have liked that." However, what the deceased once preferred or continues to prefer is not an issue (although a daughter might imagine her father sitting graveside on a cool day in autumn when the skies are clear of clouds and there is very little wind, and the father commenting, "Perfect weather for a flight out"). Tree roots greatly interfere with the digging. Root systems spread out from the trunk at least as far as its boughs spread out in the air. Therefore, begin digging beyond the farthest point of limb-spread or risk the troubling phenomenon known as *Arboreal Lament* in which injury to the roots results in a most melancholy moaning by the assaulted tree. If injury continues unchecked, the moaning will become a synchronized keening of other trees in the area. Once full-blown keening is in progress, keening trees cannot be silenced until they are cut down and destroyed in their entirety. Even the stumps and woodchips will continue to keen— though weakly—unless they are completely obliterated, so select the site with utmost care.

## Site Preparation

After the appropriate site has been selected, the surface must be inspected and prepared before the actual digging begins. There will be an assortment of rocks and stones on the site, which often shelter colonies of ants. The Old Testament holds these creatures in high esteem—"The ants are a people exceedingly wise"—Proverbs: 30: 24—and disturbance to their community should be avoided. To ascertain the presence of an ant colony, assume a prone position facing the rock you intend to lift. Tap the rock as both a warning and greeting to the vigil ant and wait five minutes (in Formic Time). This will give the colony time to prepare and summon custodial ant. Then carefully slide the blade of a kitchen knife (one taken from the household of the deceased is preferable) approximately one inch under the rock and gently pry it up. If an active colony is present, the adult custodial ant will emerge, displaying the pupa in its arms. Allow the custodial ant to withdraw, and slowly lower the rock back into position. The appearance of the adult custodial ant with young (pupae) indicates you must select a different site. If no adult/pupa appears, you may proceed with site preparation.

There will be surface vegetation to consider, including wildflowers, crabgrass, and a tangle of creepers and vines. Carefully dig these out and place in a bucket of water for replanting. Have the bucket filled and ready before you break the first earth, as you are not likely to fetch and fill a bucket in mid-dig. Once the earth is opened, the rhythm of shoveling and the dazzle of sparking stones are almost hypnotic, and you will not stop until the digging is done.

## The Surface

Knowing the size and shape of the hole will be helpful as you dig, so begin by making a surface outline two feet larger than the corpse (or coffin) on all sides, and in the shape of the burial hole you will need. Slice through the sod—the dense root matrix of grass and other plants—by using the shovel tip to make a series of small cuts with an up-and-down chopping motion. As the sod comes away from the underlying loam, gently lift it with the shovel blade, keeping it as intact as possible. Set the piece of sod aside some distance from the hole, preferably on a tarpaulin so it can be retrieved later and sprinkle it with water from your bucket. Do not scatter clumps of sod around the site willy-nilly: they will be lost in the soil that is flung from the hole.

## The Loam

Beneath the sod lies the loam layer, composed of mineral particles (sand, silt, clay) and decaying plant matter or humus (not to be confused with hummus, which is usually served with pita to those sitting *shiva* in the house of mourning, along with the usual platters of cream cheese, lox, and bagels, this last item signifying the continuity of life circling the dark hole of oblivion). Also within the loam layer you will encounter the members of the loam biota: grubs, snails, slugs, millipedes, centipedes, burrowing beetles, worms, loam lice, nematodes, and the Star-Nosed Mole (*Condylura cristata*). Do not mix the loam with other layers. Do not use your shovel to lift the loam. Instead, cautiously proceed with a spoon (traditionally runcible, but any spoon previously owned by the decedent is permissible), so you will not injure the denizens of the loam. Smaller creatures found during your spoon-work should be placed into a bucket of moist soil; the star-nosed mole should be removed and sheltered separately. He will offer no resistance to being held in your hand or gently examined, as the star-nosed species is quite tame (much like a pet white mouse that a child—a young daughter—might have kept hidden in her bedroom, and upon its escape, the father offered to the family cat). Note the mole's dense coat and his prominent snout appendages. These fleshy protuberances evolved during the Cenozoic era, when the now extinct bare-nosed mole (*Condyludra nudis*) ingested the galactic debris and star particles that fell to earth during the frequent meteor showers of that period. Modern-day meteor strikes have been attributed to star-nosed mole molestation (underground nuclear testing, hydraulic fracturing, etc.) so do not anger him. Handle/transfer the creature with care. Place him in a small, covered basket (traditionally, similar to the one that held baby Moses in the rushes—if at all possible) for safekeeping during your dig. Remember that the creatures of the loam possess mouthparts that allow them to consume decaying organic matter. After the body has been buried, they will descend and become close associates of the deceased and assist him in returning to the earth.

### The Glacial Till

The last layer of digging will be through sediment, clay, sand, and stone—the Ice Age depositions of the retreating glacier. You will also come upon rocks. Rocks, sadly, are often confused with stones. Stones are smooth, having been abraded by glacial transport. Rocks, on the other hand, are fragments of larger surface formations and not part of the glacial till. It is easy to remember which is which by the simple mnemonic: *Rough rock, smooth stone*. In addition, stones will spark and provoke a spark response in surrounding brother-stones when struck by a shovel blade. Rocks, on the other hand, will emit a low rumbling sound and smolder. Noisy rocks should be dowsed and then allowed a brief interval of rest before they are touched. Here again, your bucket will come in handy.

You will encounter larger stones that require a special excavational technique. In order to remove a large stone, wedge the tip of the shovel blade under the exposed part of it; coax it away from the surrounding soil by tilting the shovel back and forth, rocking the stone in its bed.

Remember: stones have slept undisturbed in their ancient glacial till since the Ice Age, and will be reluctant to leave the ancestral mortise. Rocks are just as difficult to dislodge, but this is due to their irregular shapes and not their disinclination to move. As with a stone, the shovel-tilt technique will release a rock from its substrate.

As the digging progresses, be sure to set aside a dozen or so stones for future use by mourners who visit. Red, brown, and blue stones are preferable and should be of a size that fits comfortably in a fisted hand. As each stone is chosen, a brief meditation is required in order to remember that the deceased is indeed lost to the living, but his soul—like a stone—will endure.

### Emergence of The *Eben-Ezer* Stones

Near the end of the digging, two stones or *Eben* will emerge. These are the "helper" or *Ezer* stones, so named in 1 Samuel 7:12: "When men of Israel smote the Philistines,

Samuel placed a stone he called Eben-Ezer between the city of Maspath and the cliffs of Sen, saying 'hitherto the Lord has helped us.'" The first *Eben-Ezer* stone will be the larger of two stones that protrude from the wall of the excavation. Its emergence signifies that the hole is not yet wide enough. You will be unable to gauge the actual size of this stone and no amount of shovel-tilting will dislodge it. Instead, position yourself prone with your chin and arms hanging over the hole and loosen it with the kitchen knife. Reach down and slide the blade between the first *Eben-Ezer* stone and its substrate, scraping away the soil as you go. You will find that it extends well past what is visible. Upon its removal, a concavity will remain; it will be necessary to remove soil all along the span of the wall, thereby automatically increasing the width of the hole. Do not be discouraged by the need for further digging. Widening of the hole at this juncture will be advantageous when you position the corpse.

After adjusting the width of the hole, continue your downward dig until a shovel-strike causes a sudden spray of sparks; this indicates that the Second *Eben-Ezer* Stone (also called the *Matzava* or *Marker Stone*) has been struck. It will be larger than any of the other stones, quite smooth, and the color of an underripe pomegranate or persimmon. Use the shovel-tilt method to free it, and place it on the surface where you will be able to easily locate it at the end of your digging. Emergence of the *Marker Stone* signifies the end of your digging, except for the leveling of the floor of the hole. This is the time to use a spirit level to ensure the floor of the hole is horizontal, so that the head and feet of the deceased will be on the same plane. If leveling off is required, make your adjustments, set the two

*Eben-Ezer* stones aside on the surface, and prepare to set the body in the hole.

### The Placement of the Body

Be sure the winding cloth is secure before placing the body in the hole. Tuck the loose ends well into a fold of the cloth to prevent the arms and legs from flopping about during descent.

Correct placement of a body is best done with two. However, if you are alone, you may place the corpse at the edge of the burial hole, position your shovel so the shaft can act as a ramp of sorts, and allow it to gently slide down. You then must climb down into the hole to make final adjustment for proper positioning: head level and in spinal alignment, face turned toward the sky, torso without tilt. When these tasks are completed, return to the surface and prepare to cover the body with soil and fill in the hole.

### Again with the Shovel

If there are other mourners, call them graveside for *K'vurah*. This act of throwing soil on the body allows them to show the deceased *Chesed Shel Emet*—a last act of compassion (although the live-in girl friend will beg off because she is afraid it might ruin her manicure, or afraid that her new shoes will be dirtied by the soil, or afraid that the daughter might smack her with the shovel). If soil from the land of Israel is available, it should be sprinkled over the body at this time.

The hole-digger should be the first and the last to put soil in the hole. The back of the shovel blade should be used to signify sadness and reluctance. Slowly, and with care and attention, throw three shovelfuls of soil upon the shrouded corpse for the three levels of the soul: *nefesh, ruach, neshama.*

Then set the shovel blade upright into the soil pile—do not hand it to the next mourner, to avoid any transfer of grief. If shoveling alone, shovel three times and rest, three times and rest, three times and rest, until all of the glacial till has been replaced. Do not be alarmed if the smaller stones spark as they are thrown into the hole. Do not be alarmed if the star-nosed mole squeaks from the shelter of his covered basket at the sound of falling soil. This behavior has been well documented, and is believed to be an expression of his anticipation in returning to his subterranean home. He will cease his squeaking when *Kaddish* has been said, as it ends with a plea for peace: *Oseh Shalom.*

Next, replace the layer of loam. Sprinkle it with water if it has dried out while you were digging. Then release the creatures of the loam biotic by allowing them to crawl from the bucket into the unpacked grave soil. When they have safely burrowed under, release the star-nosed mole from his covered basket. He will utilize his large, clawed forepaws and quickly descend. Finally, replace the sod and any surface flora previously removed, and water to help re-establish rooting.

## Setting the *Eben-Ezer* Stones

The *Eben-Ezer* stones may now be set in place, although waiting until the first *yahrzeit* is certainly permissible. Place the smaller stone at the foot and the larger one at the head. The *Matzava*, when finally inscribed, should bear the name of the deceased and nothing more.

## Dusk

The digger may choose to remain at the gravesite until after dusk to give the soul of the deceased time to become accustomed to his *beit olam*, and to finalize farewell. Sparks released from stones settling into the substrate will continue to rise from the grave and fly up into the night. It is during this somber interval that the bereaved person traditionally reflects upon events in the life of the deceased—perhaps a milestone in his life, a happy interval, or even a defining one that the bereaved person who happens to be the adult child of the deceased remembers. (Yes, sure: what a daughter would remember—a daughter, for instance—yes, the bereaved person could easily be a daughter recalling the summer night of her early childhood when she was carried to the rooftop—a very small girl lifted in her father's arms. She had settled upon his shoulder so that she could look back at the dim stairwell they ascended, and where her mother was following them up, flight after flight, until the father stopped at the top of the stairs and adjusted the child on his shoulder. He leaned into the heavy door there, sheeted in metal, riveted, creaking, and out they stepped into a world unlike the one she knew—an expanse of silhouetted smoke stacks against the night sky and distant lights shone like the closest of stars. The father set her down and she thought she might be walking on the wind, so slight and warm it came and with a smell of burning, and so darkly invisible was the blacktop floor beneath her feet, so enfolding the surrounding night. The mother pointed: there just above a far district of the city came the boom and crackle, the transient lights of the skyline pyrogenics. Sprays of blue light, and red. Pinwheels of gold. Pigeons circled over, their roosting disrupted. Clouds of colored smoke adrift. Globes exploded into silvered spiders and died. Stars shot up against gravity and whistled as they faded into the black. He had a surprise, the father told her: lights of their own—ones you could hold, ones that would crackle and sparkle on a stick. He struck a match, and held it to a magic stick. How bright it shone as it showered him with bits of light! Take one, the father said, holding it out to her. Here, he said, take it. Come on, just try. Fire! the child said. No! No! How afraid she was—such a silly child—much too afraid to hold one, and when another one was lit, the father showed her how the shower of sparks fell harmlessly upon his hands. See? he said. It doesn't hurt. Nothing to be afraid of, the father said and he lit one again, and one after another. Come on now! the mother said. Don't you trust your Daddy? But no no no, again and again, and when she was sure the last one had been lit, had sparkled itself out, fizzled all the way to the bottom of the stick, she told them: Yes, alright. Now she would hold one, now she will try. Too late! the mother scolded. All gone, the father said. Her own fault, father and mother told each other, the daughter being the child that she was: distrustful, disappointing. All gone, used up! She must cry now, she thought, and did. Stop it, the father said. Shush now, the mother said—the father having enough of it. Enough, he said and he opened up the big metal door. Take her, the mother said. You, the father said. Let's go, said the mother to the child, lifting her unmotherly, roughly; pulling her down the stairs. They put in her bed—somewhat small for her size and still with rails for someone younger, but big enough. One last one! the child cried out. Quiet now, the mother said. Shut her up, the father called from somewhere. The child turned away from the mother. The wall there was a comfort: papered in pink with white leaves and birdies on branches, lightly flocked. She liked the feel of it, the fluff of the flocking, the pictures of birdies along the branch. The light was shut. The door was slammed. She had fooled them. This, she knew, was just the start. She pressed her fingers to the papered wall and could feel the father and the mother as well, at war a room away. But the birds there still perched along her fingers. She could feel them in the dark. And that was enough.)

With dusk and the appearance of the stars, it is time to gather up the implements of digging and take leave of the gravesite. This should be done without ceremony or additional words of farewell, for all that needs to be done *has* been done. To that end, it is customary to divert ones attention from the dead and to reflect upon creation by viewing the night sky. As Isaiah 40:26 bids the mourner, "Lift up thine eyes to see the stars and who it is that calls each one by name."

Before storing away the shovel, wash away any soil that still clings to the blade. The wooden handle should be rubbed with tung oil to prevent drying and cracking. The blade should be re-sharpened with a file so it will be ready for the next usage. And it will be needed again, of course. There will always be holes to be dug, always the newly dead to be placed beside those long buried. There will always be those who lie waiting with the rocks and the stones and the lowly citizens of the loam. They will wait in the earth until the words of Isaiah 26:19 are finally spoken: "Awaken and sing, you who repose in the dust." They will wait in the earth until the earth casts out its dead. But until then, there will always be digging to be done. There will always be a time when the journeyman Soil Shifter comes 'round and is briefly considered but turned away—his services not needed. Instead, someone else will raise a foot to the rim-rest of the shovel blade, lean his weight to it and pierce the earth. Someone else will lift a shovelful of the fecund dark that all of death becomes, and begin the singular *mitzvah* that offers neither reason nor recompense.

# PARADISE FIELD

The father calls, as he does, in a voice flown away. Florida, he tells the daughter. An airstrip, he tells the girl. Look for the town of Okeechobee.

Where?—says the girl—Are you making that up? She shoves aside homework and checks her map. She flips through her book of geography.

It's east of the Gulf and west of the ocean, the father says above the static that crackles through the air.

Then home? the daughter says. Then back here?

One never can tell, the father says. And remember please: Don't tell your mother.

Don't tell her what? the daughter says.

Anything, the father says. Nothing. Not a word.

Is there something I know? the daughter says.

More than you let on, the father says.

The daughter waits for the father to call. He will call, as he does, and talk of impending weather and whether to fly home or wait for whatever's looming to lift. He will ask the daughter about changes in the wind. He will inquire about clouds.

The daughter stands at the window. She watches the trees for sway and shudder. She squints at the sky.

The father sends letters and cards, as he does, written in his bold-faced scribble.

*Hello From Oklahoma* is delivered when he's already home.

*See You Soon* arrives when he's ready to go again or he is one foot out the door.

*Greetings From Indiana.* Or Michigan. Or Missouri.

Show me, the daughter tells the mother who is sorting through the mail, finding a card tucked between pages of the penny-saver and the bills overdue.

Nothing to see, the mother says of a picture of an ocean. On the back is his jot of a note: *Hot here. Home soon.*

Where is here? the daughter says.

Floyd Bennett Field, Idlewild Airport, La Guardia, O'Hare.

The father is gone again, cloud-high in a cockpit, mixing business with pleasure. He calls home between flights, talking of sales, telling about done deals and dollars coming in. About head winds and tail winds, bad landings and bad weather.

Old familiar landscapes slip by below him. A stretch of desert with traces of an airstrip. The long-ago places he once landed war planes.

Shipped out from Sioux City at the start of the war, the father says. Or was it Wichita?

Which? says the daughter.

Like it was yesterday, the father says. Only it wasn't.

He flies over the abandoned hangars, the Quonset huts and the ruins of barracks. He sees the old bombers that he once flew now rusting on the unused runways, the tires rotting into the tarmac, weeds growing around them up to the struts.

All gone to hell, the father says.

Speaking of home, the daughter says.

Savannah, the father says in a voice that sounds happier when it's far afield. Parts south.

Which part? the daughter says.

The Old South, to be exact. Sewanee or something. I'll bring back a souvenir.

Cotton is nice, the daughter says. Get a big puff of it.

It's not so easy, the father says.

Sure, says the daughter. Sure it is. Spot a field from the air and land on a road.

How about a key chain? the father says. Or a bag of peanuts?

It's the Land of Cotton, so they've got plenty. Get the whole boll, the daughter says. The stalk and all.


Schenectady, Albany, Minneapolis, Saint Paul.

A postcard arrives with a weevil so pictured: wildly antennaed, astride a boll and strumming a banjo. The father has written: *Home tomorrow ahead of schedule.*

Ha, the mother says, tossing it in the trash, topping it with grounds from the coffee and shells from the eggs.

Fort Worth, Henderson, Duluth, Pawtucket.

A postcard arrives—a potato this time: a smiling spud astride a tractor. *Dinner*, the father has written: *Dinner, without a doubt.*

He is not home past dinner, past dark, past dawn. Morning comes with the smell of something fishy. He is at the stove, spatula in hand, fixing breakfast in a big iron skillet. Come and get it, he says, flipping canned kippers he has toted in from Calgary, scrambling eggs in over-browned butter, toasting the toast the color of carbon.

How long are you home? the mother says.

Pittsburgh next, the father says. Then Pittstown, then Pittsfield. I'll bring back coal, he tells the daughter. Bituminous and funnel cakes.

The daughter waits, as she does, for the father to call. She stands in the yard looking at the sky. It is bright, and the light is abundant despite the lateness of the day. The objects of the yard stand in their dailyness, unshadowed, unordinary: stones rowed and chunked along the drive, leaves unraked and windblown in the corners of the steps. The girl, too, so illuminated, so plain in the unforgiving light as she walks throughout the yard in her rambling, graceless step. Her hands across her brow against the severity of sky. Her hands are unpretty, too: roughened, coarse, older than she is—hands of a girl who likes newly dug holes and what crawls or hides under stones; the hands of a girl who likes weeds left unchecked in the straggly yard and wasps in the paint-peeled eaves and birds nesting in the uncut shrubbery; a girl who likes shells and shards and the smash of a hammer that splits the shale, reveals the imprints of bivalves that lived when the world was an ocean and the sky rained a millennium of rain.

Hurricane, Reading, Moab, Little Rock.

Trilobites would be nice, the daughter says. Where you are, they've got lots.

It's not so easy, the father says.

Sure it is, the daughter says. Stop at a road-cut or the edge of a canyon. Chip it from a cliff.

Come home with a piece of something old in your pocket.

Syracuse, Missoula, Halifax, Mesquite.

It's your father, shouts the mother of the girl, her head stuck out the upstairs window. Your father's on the phone. Talk to your father.

Where are you? says the daughter.

El Paso today, the father says, Laredo tomorrow. Where the skies are not cloudy all day.

And then? says the daughter. Then where will you be?

That's up in the air and up for discussion, he says, where he will be will not be home and will not be headed.

He will not be in the yard, trimming the hedge or pushing the mower or watering the lawn the way other fathers are seen to do up and down the block. He will not be in the bathroom having a shave and running the tap. Not in the kitchen frying hash in the cast iron skillet. Not in the living room sleeping on the sofa where he sometimes sleeps or in the big cherrywood bed in the bedroom upstairs where the mother rests with the television always running: *Queen for a Day* and *Curse of the Mummy*, flickering like lightning of a summer storm coming or a late afternoon squall on its way.

Montgomery, home. Home, Fargo.

~

The father stops at home before heading somewhere colder. He is in the downstairs closet, pitching out clothes, tripping over overshoes and vacuum cleaner hoses. Tossing aside hats.

He is looking for the jacket he wore in the war, the genuine leather now hidden in the attic. Left breast insignia, regulation zipper. Mice in the lining. Moths in the pocket flaps.

This house, this goddamn house, the father says from a hollow of coats.

Packed to the rafters with crap, he says, under a cascade of hangers.

The daughter is there by the closet door. She can hear the father's voice from the closed-in dark. It is muffled by mufflers, by windbreakers and raincoats. Quieted by over-coats and winter coats. Hardly heard anymore in the winters going by, the seasons in flight.

The father is gone, flying to parts far-flung. Old familiar landscapes are slipping below him. He is post-war now and piloting alone—solo over forests of Ponderosa Pine and Pinyon, the desert outposts of the Mojave and Sonora, the heartland croplands and the living hills—high above the old airdromes long missing from maps and places that have been phased out of flight plans: Far City Station, Gardenia Corps Depot, Paradise Field. He is far from home and hearth, from cinders in the fireplace, from creosote in the chimney. He is taking a break from breaking crockery during kitchen quarrels, an R&R from slamming bedroom doors and splitting lintels. He has taken his leave from shoveling snow, from shoving and snarling and smashing and seething. He has flown away from spats, fights, and home front skirmishes. He has left the lawn mower clotted with sod and the garden hose tangled. The kiddy pool seeps in a yard turned to swamp. The gutters overflow with rotted leaves. The water heater has filled with silt. It rumbles whenever a faucet is opened, sizzling along a faulty seam unseen.

The wife—the mother of the girl—holds up the phone when the father calls. Here, she tells the daughter, you take this call. Ask your father if he'll reveal his whereabouts.

Ask him yourself, the daughter says.

George dear, says the mother of the girl—the wife—to the husband on the phone. Would you be so kind? Would it be an imposition? May I ask where you are?

Hard to say, the father says. Just might need to take a train if they're not allowing take-offs.

And when are you back? the mother says. We were just wondering. The toilet's clogged. The sump pump isn't sumping. We have squirrels in the attic. The cat is missing.

There's a client to talk to out in Missoula, the father tells her. And I've got a deal going in Paducah.

A likely story—she shouts into the phone—but of course the wife is the last to know.

Know what? the father says.

And here's another thing: You missed dinner, she says. If you must know, I cooked a chicken.

Freeze it, the father says. Or can it. Either.

I'm done, says the mother as she hands the girl the phone. Here—she says—Talk.

Daddy, says the girl, taking the phone. Is that you?

Who else? the father says.

~

There are delays due to rain. Precipitation is imminent.
Word trickles in:

A postcard postmarked Big Sky Country:

>A cactus waving and wearing a cowboy hat.
>*See you later.*
>*Your Daddy.*

A postcard postmarked Land of Enchantment:

>A two-headed calf.
>*Think it's a fake?*
>*Love, Daddy.*

A card from The Greater Twin Cities:

>*Passing over home Sunday noon.*
>*Will tilt wings. Look up.*
>*Guess who.*

A note on a card postmarked Paradise Field:

>Abandoned remains of tumbleweed runway.
>And written below it, in his usual scribble:
>*X marks the spot where I was while there was a war.*

Didn't you hear me? the mother says. Get in here, she says,
holding the phone.

Get out there, says the father to the daughter. Take a look
at the sky.

I'm looking right now, the daughter tells him. I'm at the
window and I'm looking.

No good—not the window, the father says. Go stand in the yard that I'm supposed to be mowing. Stand in the weeds that I'm not pulling up.

The daughter looks at the sky, trying to make sense of it: so abundantly dull, so faultlessly white. Nimbostratus? Rain much later? Wisps of clouds are lifting like smoke along the horizon. Shreds of clouds are sliding above the rooftops, the treetops, and the chimneys. Cottony clouds are tugged from the bottles of medicinals kept on the bathroom shelf: the aspirin for the mother's headache, the Alka-Seltzer for the father's hangover. The daughter flips open caps and digs out clouds: a fluffy clump of cotton for a cumulonimbus. Wispy strands for cirrus. She keeps specimens of clouds pasted on cardboard, displayed and named with notes on the weather. Tuesday: Cirrus. Two inches of snow. Wednesday: Stratus. Chance of rain.

Chesterfield, Warwick, Raleigh, Worchester. The father is gone, and going somewhere else.

Where? The daughter says.

Delray, the father says. Then Miami.

Moon shells are nice, the daughter says. Whelks, too. I could use a whelk for my collection. I could hang them from strings so they'd float in the air.

It's not all beach, the father says. It's New York with palm trees so it's not so easy.

Sure it is, the daughter says. After a storm there's lots of stuff. Go at low tide. Check the flotsam. I'll make a wind chime. I'll hang it in the window.

Listen, says the father. They're patching me in. Can you hear the engine? The buzz of the turbo props?

I sort of hear something, the daughter says. It sounds like the sea.

Cockles from Ocean City, a whelk from Delray.

The father is gone and not going anywhere, held up at the edge of a front.

Fogged in, he tells the daughter, phoning from the edge of a city. Big delays. The westerly winds are reversing direction. Tell your mother don't hold dinner and don't wait up.

You tell her, the daughter says.

Shit, the father says.

What now? says the mother, taking the phone.

Bad weather, says the father.

I'll just bet, says the mother.

Socked in, says the father.

Even better, says the mother.

La Baja, Tijuana, the father says.

Let me talk, says the daughter. Let me tell him.

Make it fast, the father says.

Bring beans, the daughter says. The ones that jump in the heat of your hand. Keep them safe until you're home, until you actually come through the door.

Kansas City, Little Rock, Wichita.

And corn—bring corn, the daughter says. Remember, Daddy: the kind you pop.

The father is gone. He calls when he calls. He comes home when he does, or when the wind is right.

Go outside and check the sky, he says. Tell me what I'll be flying into.

There's no sun, the daughter says, but everything is bright.

Clouds? the father says.

Stratus, the daughter says. Growly and low, like something might fall.

Chicken little, the father says.

Rain, I expect, the daughter says. Will you be back for dinner?

In case of rain, the father says, don't expect me.

Where are you, Daddy? the daughter says.

Guess, says the father.

I won't, the daughter says.

I'll give you a hint, the father says. Here it is: It's warm.

If it's California, the daughter says, bring back a nugget. Sutter's Mill is somewhere there.

Not so easy, says the father.

Sure it is. Look for something sparkly.

Guess again, the father says. There's a hole filled with water.

Crater Lake, the daughter says. Find a meteorite.

Or a crescent of moon. Or a moon shell or whelk.

Listen, the father says, and you'll hear the ocean.

The daughter holds the moon shell to her ear. But she hears the hum inside a fuselage and the roar of the airstream over a wing.

A whelk shell hangs on a hook in her window. (From the beach at Delray, or was it Hyannis?)

A stone sits forgotten in a corner on the shelf. (Found in Philadelphia. Or Cheyenne. Or possibly Fargo.)

The father is gone. He is moving through the air.

# THE RENOIR IS PUT STRAIGHT

*L'Auberge.* The sign can be seen from the road. *The child will remember the vine that winds around the post. She will remember the willow in the yard.*

The cottages are clapboard. The main house and the stairs to the dining room are stone. The dining room windows face east. A Renoir print hangs above the table where they always sit. *Girl With Watering Can.* The frame is gilt.

Breakfast is omelette au fromage, sometimes with a sprinkling of chervil. One of the guests—was it Madame Larouche?—heard that Chef Henri may surprise everyone with omelette aux truffes one day this week.

A basket covered with a cloth holds the warm baguette. The butter is sweet. A clot of jam sits in a dish. The mother tells the child that it is cherry, although it is cassis. But this is something that the child does not believe.

~

Most tables have a view: the lawn, the court for la boule, the swimming pond.

An orchard can be seen from the kitchen. The trees are bent and untended. Birds, undisturbed, make their nests. The unpicked apples—sooty with blight—fall and rot.

*The child will remember the sweet smell of ferment, the tunnels in the browning folds of grass, and once—a glimpse of a traveling mouse.*

The dining room is clean but has a well-worn look. The floorboards are wide and dark. The tablecloths are white.

Ah. Here comes Madame Ménage with her tray of flowers—rushing as usual, table to table, before Chef Henri Ménage rings the breakfast bell. Madame favors yellow: buttercups in summer and goldenrod in the fall when most guests are gone.

Hop clover grows around the cottages and all along the road. The flowers are furred like the feet of the rabbits in the hutch behind the kitchen: the brown one and the all-white one and the one nearly as blue as slate. The child pets them though the mesh-wire. Chef Henri Ménage tells her that she must never pick them up. They hate to be held, he says—they'll only claw and kick. But the child does not believe Chef Henri Ménage.

*The child will remember the morning Chef Henri carried his stick to the hutch behind the kitchen. And that he hung all three—the brown one, the one all-white, the one as blue as slate—limp and dripping from the kitchen rack, beside the copper pots. She will remember the big hooks sunk into their flanks. The pan beneath. She will remember the word lapin to mean something to be held in one's lap.*

At last: here is Chef Henri Ménage, emerging from his kitchen, barging though the old screen door. He stands on the landing at the very top step. He looks out at the fields and the mist above from the swimming pond. He looks down at the guests milling about below him on the lawn, chatting about the weather and their plans for the day. Il fait froid ce matin! Did you hear that rain last night? Après manger: le ping-pong or la boule—which?

Chef Henri leans to the rail and clangs his big square bell over them, as if he does not see them, as if they are all still in bed. Everyone looks up and shouts—Henri! Henri!—and covers their ears with their hands. Everyone laughs.

*Who will remember the sound of Chef Henri's bell? The child—the girl—will hear it in her dreams.*

The guests climb the stone stairs. They greet the mother and the father and the child on their way up: Bonjour Hirschbergers! Bonjour Pamela!

What do you say? the mother says, and gives the child's hand a yank.

The child is somewhat shy of them, ungraceful in her clothes: blouse partly tucked, socks mismatched, one down, one up. And is that a twig stuck in her hair where it is coming undone?

Here come the Rogets in their matching straw hats. Bonjour Hirschbergers! And how is la jeune fille?

Here is Philippe Bouvier with his bird-glasses around his neck. Madame et Monsieur et Pamela—Comment allez-vous?

Now Mademoiselle Karine with her old Papa Frederick. Bonjour Bonjour! says Mademoiselle Karine.

Frederick stops to tip his cap.

Claudia Larouche carries her little dog Pierre. Woof woof, says Claudia Larouche to anyone who will look. *The child will remember that pierre means stone; she will always think of it as an odd name for a dog.*

Here is Monsieur Diage stomping up with his oak-knot cane. Excusez-moi, he says and everyone makes way.

The child is told to stop to let him pass, and to please retie her shoes properly so the laces will not come loose.

Next are the Bernards—Monsieur and Madame with their baby Chappell wrapped in his blanket, his face peeping out.

Now here comes Monsieur Martin Morey helping along his little Mama Jacqueline. *The child will remember that Jacqueline smelled of lavender and pee.*

Bonjour Pamela, say the old sisters Paulette and Pauline Baptiste holding tightly to the rail with each tottering step. The child is told to move out of the way.

Now the Durants. Bonjour Americans!

Now the Dubonnets. Bonjour!

*Everyone will remember the night a doe and fawn walked onto the court for la boule. The Durants and the Dubonnets were on their knees, measuring the marks in the sand and arguing the shot. They did not see the doe and fawn pass behind their back as they measured the distance to the cochonnet. They did not hear the other guests fall silent. They did not see the doe and fawn walk under the bright bulbs strung post to post or how the doe held up her small stony hoof in hesitation before the next step. They did not see them slip back into the wood.*

Everyone is clattering into the dining room now, talking on about this and that. Let's hope baby Chappell won't start up. Sure sure, un bébé charmant—but he'd better not. Philip Bouvier says he heard a nightingale at dusk. Does Madame Larouche have that dog on a leash? I am sure the Ménages get complaints. Did you hear?—Chef Henri is planning his tarragon potatoes with tonight's entrée. Where is that André? I need my café.

Everyone is taking their usual seats.

Mademoiselle Karine tucks a napkin under her Papa Fredrick's neck. Ouch, he says—too tight.

Claudia Larouche pats an empty seat. Pierre wiggles his haunches and hops up.

Monsieur Bernard lifts baby Chappell and wags his arm to have him wave.

Martin Morey and his little Mama Jacqueline take their table near the door so she hasn't far to walk.

Now the old sisters Baptiste. There is always great commotion when they sit, both being quite deaf. J'ai froid! shouts Pauline Baptiste. There's a draft! shouts Paulette. They loudly scrape their chairs along the floor. They bump the table. Drop spoons. Shh, says Monsieur Bernard. Baby Chappell begins a stint of chin-quivering—a deceptive delay—then opens his mouth and howls. Pierre lifts his head and bays.

Monsieur Diage raps the floor with his oak-knot cane. Mon Dieu!—ça sufit!

Arrête! says Philippe Bouvier. He sits and opens his bird-guide to *Birds In Silhouette*. Philippe Bouvier is working on his life list.

Madame Jardine sniffs the buttercups that Madame Ménage has arranged, though she knows they have no scent.

Madame and Monsieur Roget do not remove their straw hats.

Now here are the Durants.

Now the Dubonnets.

The child follows the father and the mother to the corner table, under the Renoir print. She sits on a pillow to reach table height.

And here is André—here to serve—arriving unsummoned. He steps astutely tableside, bearing saucers stacked in his arm-crook and cup-handles hooked on his fingers. The towel he folds waiter-style on his arm is unwrinkled, unstained. His gold wire glasses glint. He sets the crockery in place without so much as a rattle or clink. André sees past all pathetic pleasantries. He does not pander, engage. He is unmoved by friendly attempts.

*André will remember the August afternoon he stood on the kitchen back-step, shaking out the tablecloths after serving the lunch. He will re-member looking up the slope and seeing the child—what was her name?—sitting in the orchard, her back against a tree, her arms crossed around her knees—and watching him lift and snap the tablecloths over the rail and up in the air. He will remember that he thought to wave—but he did not—nor did she. Many years hence André will think of this as a nurse spoons soup into his mouth.*

Paulette Baptiste tells sister Pauline that Chef Henri
Ménage has made pain au raisin today. What? What? shouts
Pauline Baptiste. Pain au raisin! Pain au raisin! The other
guests lift the cloths that cover their baskets of bread to look.
But no: the usual plain baguette.

André is back. He gazes at the wall just over their heads.
He speaks. Pardonnez-moi, André says, with the faint scowl
of noting something amiss. The mother and the father slightly quake. André sidles into the narrow space between the wall
and the child in her chair. He leans over. He is just above
her head. He is stepping closer in, closer than when he sets
down a platter or arranges the cutlery or makes a space for
the tureen of soup. The child sits very still, her hands in her
lap. She slides down in her seat, somewhat under the flap of
tablecloth. She is a small thing, quiet and hiding in the folds
of browning grass. She is a wind-pummeled heart, an apple shaken loose and thudding to earth. André is closer still.
André reaches in. His hand near the wall now, just over her
head. Ah, the print! The Renoir is atilt! He reaches up and
puts it straight.

André now steps back to check: the graveled garden path,
the watering can, and the subject—a girl with hair the color of
spun honey. The crimson ribbon. The velvet dress. The frame
of gilt. Much better, the father says. Yes, very good, the mother
says. The child looks. *Girl With Watering Can.* No resemblance,
the mother says. Not one bit.

~

47

André makes his usual slight bow. Monsieur, Madame, he says. He will be returning soon with the omelettes—perhaps aux truffes? And please—they would like to say—some café au lait when you get a chance. Though everyone knows better than to actually ask André.

Here comes Madame Ménage, table-to-table, greeting the guests. And here she is tableside. Bonjour Hirschbergers! says Madame Ménage. The father beams. The mother does not.

André is on his way, says Madame Ménage. In the meantime, is there anything that you need?

Well yes, the father says, and winks.

Monsieur! What do you mean? says Madame Ménage feigning innocence. Le Can Can? she says. Le danse de Moulin Rouge? and she two-handedly lifts her skirt to just above her knees and gives the hem a left-right swish. Voilà! she says, with a saucy little kick.

Bravo, the father says.

Merci Monsieur! says Madame Ménage, dancing off.

She has some nerve—the mother says—for a woman of ill repute. You'd think she'd keep it to herself.

Oh hell, the father says. Don't start.

The mother whispers to the child: They didn't wear their underpants on stage at the Moulin Rouge.

The father is smiling, sheepish. He bends to the child and sings softly in her ear: Oh they don't wear underpants in the southern part of France.

Stop, the mother says.

You, the father says.

Wouldn't she feel cold on a windy day? asks the child.

No—she wouldn't, the father says. Absolutely not.

But this is something that the child does not believe.

The child asks the father if he would come with her for a walk. Daddy please. She knows a spot in the stream by the bridge where there are tiny fishes—shiny like pins.

Is that so? the father says.

Yes and also a shady place where a bird has a nest.

You don't say, the father says.

Oh yes and also a broken dolly in the dirt.

And where was this? the father says.

Across the road in a ditch in a field where the man has a plough.

You went where? the mother says. Just where did you say you went?

The child does not say that after yesterday's lunch—co-quilles Saint-Jacques—she went up the slope all by herself and sat in the orchard and picked a rotting apple out of the browning folds of grass and took a taste.

She does not say that after last night's dessert—mousse au chocolate—she went alone past the court for la boule, through the swinging gate, along the cornfield path, and over the little bridge where the fish are silver pins. And that she went carefully along the banks of the swimming pond to the shallow end where the swimmers never swim. That there she saw stars making circles in the water and a snail on a rock and a frog jumping in and a snake that went sliding away through the watergrass—and she saw the slow underwater whip of its dark-patterned body and its glossy head held just above the surface unplaiting the blades of yellow-green watergrass and bearing behind it the wave of its body, the wave-on-wave of it, a ribbon of grace. No, she does not say.

She does not say that she saw Monsieur Diage try to smash a spider with his cane on the dining room stone stairs but he missed and the spider ran away and hid in a crack and Monsieur Diage said: Aha! Got it!—even though he didn't, and anyway—she never believes anything Monsieur Diage has to say.

Fish like pins, the child says again. So can we please?
Well, the father says.
Fix yourself, the mother tells the child. You missed a button.

Ah. Here is André, returning now with two chrome pots.

The child watches him with quiet intent. The way he pours the coffee and milk together, the liquids streaming out of their respective spouts. The up-and-down filling of the cups. How he keeps the towel folded on his forearm, elbow bent. How he gazes slightly over his gold wire glasses and tilts his head so that she sees there the silver of the pots. And she sees how he does not drip or make a mess. How he does not bring a pen or pad to write. How he does not look at her in her misbuttoned dishevelment.

André now collects a soiled spoon and an unneeded dish. His bearing hints at mild disgust; his slight nod and bow suggests that he means to insult. Old school, the father says when

André turns evenly on his heel and heads for the kitchen door with its round window near the top and the brass nail heads all around the rim.

The door swings in: kitchen sounds of pot-lids and sizzle. Chef Henri Ménage there at the great hooded stove in the bright steamy light. His round belly crisscrossed with apron ties wound back to front. *The child will remember his hat as a white stalk with a pouf of cloud on top.* He shakes a pan above the grate. Flames leap.

The door swings in. Madame slipping inside, calling: Henri! The door swings out. André slipping back out, balancing platters.

Here comes André. He sets down his platters. He lifts the silver domed lids that keep in the heat, and quickly turns them up to catch the beads of condensation before they drip.

The child tests the china rim with a fingertip. She wonders how André can hold what she can barely touch—what would burn her, it is so hot.

Her hands—she knows—are not like the *Girl With Watering Can*. No resemblance. Not a bit. Her fingers—she knows—are stupid and thick. There is grit in her nails, a twig in her hair, a found piece of bone in her pocket. She is a child who peeks under rocks, who likes the millipede that rolls into a perfect sphere when touched.

~

Sit up, the mother says.

Did you wash your hands? the father says. Did you use soap?

Madame reappears. Her again—the mother of the child mumbles while feigning occupation with the buttering of the baguette. Cows are dull but they do make butter, the mother has told the child—but these are things that the child does not believe.

Excusez! says Madame Ménage. Bad news! Today the swimming pond will be drained. It has been years—how many?—since it was dredged and the spring was re-dug. There is too much silt. And even worse: a snake was sighted by the sisters Baptiste! Poor dears, they had to end their swim. The Durants and the Dubonnets say it is large, but it may have been just been a stick. Claudia Larouche fears it will attack her dog Pierre. And Philippe Bouvier saw it slither from the water and swallow a fledgling bluebird on the spot! And the Bernards—they have a small baby to protect. So. The snake must be routed out.

Ah. André is just now passing by. One might desire a bit more café. But, no. Too late. He has decided that everyone has had enough.

But do not worry, continues Madame Ménage. Other recreation has been arranged. A mushroom walk—we pick des champignons—two pastures past the swimming pond. Where the cows—how do you say—make excrement? She pinches her nose with her fingers—merde, she says. Kaka, she tells the child and hoping the child will laugh. It is the best time for champignons, now that we have had a good rain.

Would Pamela like to come?, inquires Madame Ménage. Would the little one like to learn which champignons are good to eat, sauté avec un peu de la beurre—she kisses her fingertips—and which are les anges de mort?

*The child will remember that ange is angel and that mort is short for Uncle Morty who is dead.*

Mademoiselle Karine will come along with us and bring her Papa Frederick, says Madame Ménage.

Frederick is our Mushroom Man, our expert, she says.

Claudia Larouche will bring Pierre, who promises not to bark.

Madame Roget will come, but Monsieur Roget will stay to drain the pond and dig.

Philippe Bouvier will walk with us and name the birds.

Madame Jardine will point out which are wildflowers and which are weeds.

Monsieur Diage will not come. He cannot walk far, even with his cane.

Monsieur Bernard will stay behind and work. Madame must mind baby Chappell.

Martin Morey will come along; he likes to walk. His Mama Jacqueline remains here for her nap.

Our Chef Henri will supervise the dredging and the opening of the lock.

And the Durants and the Dubonnets? They prefer a game of la boule, of course. They are already making bets!

~

Ah, here comes the mushroom group straggling across the lawn. Baskets, knapsack, kerchiefs. Martin Morey in hiking boots. Madame Roget in her usual straw hat. All talking. Wait up. Where's the corkscrew? Who has the food? Did Chef Henri pack a knife? The child is taken by the hand. Pamela, where's your hat?—and she is given a hat. They pass the court for la boule. Now through the swinging gate. They follow the path through the field of corn that seems to make its own waves of heat. Next the plank bridge. Over the stream where the fish are silver pins. High grass. Stone path. Swimming pond.

The men are already at work, digging the bottom out. The iron lock is up. The water is flowing away. A rim of flat stones marks were the water was, where the swimming pond has shrunk away from the grassy banks.

Chef Henri stands in the pit. He still wears his apron tied around front and his sleeves rolled to elbow length. Monsieur Bernard is hauling out debris. The father of the child slings away a shovelful of mud. Monsieur Roget takes off his straw hat and fans his face. Monsieur Diage is on the bank with his cane, smacking at frogs trying to escape.

A turtle washes against the lock, green with algae and as big as a platter. Chef Henri snatches it up by the tail and holds it at arm's length. The neck twists, jaws snap. Inside its mouth is white. The frantic fanning of its feet. La Soupe de tortue? says Chef Henri. Everyone shouts: Oui, Henri! La Soupe de tortue!

The child is lifted over the stream that flows out past the iron lock. The father waves: Be good, Pamela.

Here is the next field. Wet meadow. Dim, cool wood. Sun shifting though the leaves, light spattering the path. A peeping in a bough. A distant whistle. Philippe Bouvier, in the lead, puts up his hand for everyone to stop. Claudia Larouche is looking down at what Pierre has in his mouth and she bumps into the back of Martin Morey who knocks against Philippe Bouvier who tells everyone to pay attention, s'il vous plaît! He points overhead. Crested flycatcher—announces Philippe Bouvier—mais…c'est trop petit—so possibly a wren. All look up into the fluttering leaves, a play of sun and green. They crane their necks, squint. Where? says Claudia Larouche. I don't see it, says Mademoiselle Karine. Oh my neck, says her old Papa Frederick. Where? says Martin Morey. Where?

No one hurries. No one hurries the child along when she stops to pick things up: butterfly wing, wood beetle, hickory nut. No one hastens Madame Jardine when she stops to gather asters for a small bouquet.

Claudia Larouche and Mademoiselle Karine sing Je Chante! and skip and dance along the path. Pierre howls, joins in. Shh—you'll scare the birds! says Philippe Bouvier.

~

Now here is the hedgerow, a log to climb over, the end of the path. A rusted wire fence is held up. One by one, all duck under. They step out of the dim wood and into the sunlit pasture—a green expanse—the grass close-cropped. Here and there is a thorny shrub and a thistle that the cows have spared. And the champignons—the champignons! They are everywhere—pale as rounds of leftover snow, bright as a scattering of stones.

Monsieur Frederick instructs: See the caps? he says. No spots. And underneath the gills are white. He sniffs. La odeur— he says—de la terre.

Madame Jardine points out a pasture rose. Pierre pisses on a dried pile of dung. The baskets fill with champignons. Ah, let's see what out Pamela has picked. Monsieur Frederick examines the cap, the color of the gills, and the shape of the stalk. Oui! Look everyone! Our Pamela has found the biggest one.

The baskets fill. Time for lunch.

They open the knapsack and spread a cloth. Baguette. Fromage de chèvre. Red pear. Chocolate bar. Chablis Grands Cru—still quite cool—is poured into small tin cups. The child is given a taste. Hmmm, says Martin Morey—a hint of framboise, he says, with a faint undertone of oak. Mademoiselle Karine chokes and laughs. Madame Roget squirts chablis out her nose. Slices of pear are handed off on the blade of the knife. Philippe Bouvier spots a warbler—or is it a vireo? Sips of wine. Sun overhead. The cover of kerchiefs and hats. They sleep in the grass.

~

Come Pamela, says Mademoiselle Karine. Time to wake up, says Madame Roget.

The cores of the pears are tossed away. The cups are drained, packed up. The knife is wiped clean and wrapped. Grass is shaken from the cloth. Oh my knees, says Monsieur Frederick.

It is cooler now as they again step under the wire fence and set off through the wood. Longer shadows in the hedgerow trees. First firefly. Early crickets. Monsieur Bouvier spots a hawk but keeps quiet. Field, field, stone wall, wet meadow. Up ahead, they can see the other guests stand beside the swimming pond on the bank. Well look at that. Everyone is there, it seems. Even the Durants and the Dubonnets—they must have finished their match. And see, Pamela—Voilà!—there's your mother. And Madame Bernard with baby Chappell. Even Mama Jacqueline, up from her nap. Everyone now at the drained swimming pond, everyone watching the men down in the pit. Chef Henri stands in the mud, wielding a stick. Get it! Tuez-le! shouts Chef Henri.

The snake swims—a frantic undulation—in the small black pool that is left. Chef Henri is up to his knees in the muck. He takes a step. The snake slips under, gone. Everyone waits. Its head comes up. It rises for a breath. Tuez-le! screams Pauline Baptiste. Tuez-le! shouts Paulette. Monsieur Bernard thrusts a rake. Chef Henri jabs his stick into the mud. Monsieur Bernard goes into the pit with a shovel. Now

Martin Morey. The snake squirms in the thick silt. Smash. Smash. The skin breaks. The wound is pink. An avulsion of its strange pale flesh. Still it slides away from them through the small circle of water that is left. Monsieur Bernard snatches the stick from Chef Henri. Now Philippe Bouvier joins in. Now Claudia Larouche. Old Papa Fredrick falls in the mud but manages to give the snake a whack. It struggles through the slime, trying to reach the bank as Madame Jardine drops her flowers and pitches a rock. Vite, vite! says Papa Frederick. Il se sauve! The father of the child pries loose a rock and lifts it two-handedly over his head and brings it down. The snake is hit and slips into the dark water but starts out again. Monsieur Diage brings down his cane. Smack. Smack. Still it writhes in the broken blades of watergrass, its head pulling what is left of the living length of it along, dragging the broken remains. Tuez-le, say the sisters Baptiste. Now Chef Herni with a final strike. Finalement. He lifts the body on his stick. He holds it up for everyone to see. Flayed now. Broken. Hooray for Henri! Hooray. Hooray. Now to the wire fence, to hang it on a barb. Pierced there, displayed. Hooray. But look. Is it not dead? See that? It moved? Il n'st pas mort! screams Mama Jacqueline, as it slightly lifts its head. More stones! shouts Claudia Larouche. Fracassez-le! The father of the child has the stick and does his work. Now the mother of the child strikes once, twice. And again. Monsieur Bernard holds baby Chappell so Madame Bernard can throw a stone. She grazes its head. Bon coup! Now the Rogets. Now the Dubonnets. And now the Durants. Yes, yes! A turn for everyone! A tear, a rent. A blow on blow. The sun is setting. A spill of pink. The sleek head still intact. Splinter of spine. Everyone claps, everyone cheers. *The child will remember the word for blood: sang sang sang, sang sang sang.*

Chef Henri is laughing—see how his apron is spattered with mud. Henri! What a mess! And see Papa Frederick— Frederick, you're soaking wet! The men all shake each other's hands, slap each other on their backs. Everyone is talking and laughing as they head up the slope. Over the plank bridge. Along the stone path. Cornfield. Through the gate. Chef Henri hurries ahead. He is sure that André has the tables ready and that he has set out the tureens. He is sure Madame Ménage has kept the soup at a simmer, but he still must add a sprinkling of basil. He still has to add a bit more tarragon to the potatoes. He still has to pipe the buttercream decoration on the hazelnut gâteau. He must hurry. Madame Ménage will be wondering. And André—he's bound to be annoyed, having to serve dinner so late.

*André will die one night as his nurse puts him to bed. She will lift and flap his sheet to shake off the crumbs from his beard and the bits of food that have missed his mouth. The sheet will rise and billow above him, will float down and cover him, and he will think of the child in the orchard who sat in the browning folds of grass, the child who watched him shake the tablecloths, and he will wonder again—what was her name?—and he will remember—it will come to him: Pamela. Her name was Pamela. Yes, that was it.*

Chef Henri goes to the rail: a quick clang-clang. The dinner bell at last. Everyone climbs the big stone steps. Everyone is talking as they take their usual seats. What a day!

I'm starved to death. What are we having? Chef Henri hinted at lapin tourtière. I heard lamb and ratatouille. Where's that André?

Too tight, says Old Papa Frederick when Madame Karine sticks a napkin under his collar. La boule tonight? Ping-pong? say the Durants. No no—it's just too late, say the Dubonnets. This isn't my wine, announces Martin Morey. I've got yours! calls Philipe Bouvier. Then where's mine? says Monsieur Roget. Woof, says Madame Larouche. Waaah, says baby Chappell. Shh, say the Bernards. Shh, says Monieur Diage. What was that? shouts Pauline Baptiste. The dog! shouts Paulette.

*The dog—Pierre—will be killed the coming fall while running unleashed, shot by a hunter who mistook him for a fox. Claudia Larouche will have him mounted with one paw up.*

*Claudia Larouche will die of an infection that blackens her foot. The remains of Pierre will be thrown in the trash.*

*Monsieur Diage will fall one day despite his cane, sustaining a blow to the back of his neck.*

*The sisters Baptiste will live on for many years, but will not remember that they are sisters or each other's names.*

*Old Frederick will die on a windy afternoon while chasing after his cap. His daughter, Mademoiselle Karine, will fall from a great height.*

~

*Monsieur Martin Morey will die before his little Mama Jacque-line—a problem with his heart. Mama Jacqueline will cough and break a vessel in her lung.*

*Baby Chappelle Bernard will develop a fever of the brain and die in his crib. Madame and Monsieur Bernard will part.*

*Madame and Monsieur Roget will go to separate homes for the in-firm. They will not be permitted to wear their straw hats.*

*Chef Henri will die long after he shuts L'Auberge for good—a prob-lem in the gut, discovered too late. Madame Ménage will call the old guests to tell them he is dead: Hello?—she will say—Madame Hirschberger? This is Madame Ménage! I am calling with news about my dear Hen-ri!—But the mother of the child will not speak with Madame Ménage.*

*The Durants and the Dubonnets will die in a boating accident on the Seine.*

*The deer will die in a late-winter storm.*

*Monsieur Philippe Bouvier will have 388 birds on his life list.*

Ah. Here is André with the soup. He glances at the Renoir print that hangs above the table. *Girl With Watering Can.* André is a bit perturbed tonight—put upon, to be exact—to be serving at this hour. The child yawns. Sit up, the father says. Goodness— says the mother—just look at those hands. Did you even wash, did you use any soap? André makes room for the tureen with the silver lid. His gold wire glasses cloud with the brief rise of steam—then clear—as he lifts the cover off. Magnifique: bisque of tomato provençale with fresh basil—just a touch. Comments now from all around: Oui, très bon! Délicieux! And the basil—just right. It needed more pepper, calls out Martin Bouvier as he wipes his mouth. No it didn't, says Claudia Larouche. But where is the entree? J'ai faim! What is Chef Henri doing out there? Mon Dieu, but that André is awfully slow tonight!

The mother tells the child: Fix your napkin. Finish your soup.

*The child—Pamela—will grow and live, and live as people do. Her mother—though frail—will persevere.*

*Her father will die first. She will visit him in the evenings in the years that mark her middle life; she will sit beside his bed, cut his food, help him eat. She will say goodnight. She will be called one morning and informed that he is dead—that he died in his sleep—peacefully, as they say. But that part of it—that one part of it—will be something she does not believe.*

Here comes André, returning with the meal. Finalement! He sets down the big platter. He lifts the silver dome with the slightest flourish of his wrist. Voilà! But what is this? Ah! You see! Chef Henri never disappoints. It is not lapin tourtiere, oh no. But even better—and a surprise for all—medallions of veal with champignons en croûte!

And of course—those tarragon potatoes that everyone likes.

*Madame Ménage will die soon after her Chef Henri.*
*No one will recall that she once danced on the stage of the Moulin Rouge.*

# THE SONG INSIDE THE PLATE

The corner seat is where I sit. Sissy sits by the window. Father sits so no one can get out. The kitty is under the table where the floor has a bump. Sometimes the kitty stands on two back feet just like a person stands. Mother stands. She goes where the stove is or walks around and carries dishes. Sissy keeps her lamb in her lap. Where his hair is gone away Mother made a patch. Sissy pets the patch. She always lifts the lamb up to sniff the pieces on her plate. The monkey stays in bed because he does not like to sniff. The radio is on. A man talks with a voice slowed down. The man says: *Speaking of sports.* Father says: Shush. The man says: *Whoa. Right cross.* Mother slams the lids of pots. Father says: Didn't I say shush? Didn't I? The man says: *How about that left hook?* Mother hits the potatoes in the pot. The man says: *He's down for the count.* Father says: All right. Father goes to the drawer where Mother keeps the big fork. The drawer is stuck. Father says: This house. Father pulls the drawers and they fall out. Mother turns around. The car went in the yard. The yard was mud where the roses were and where we put the stone. The big pole came down. Mud came in the house. There were sparks and wires like snakes. Sissy hit her mouth. I hurt my foot. My shoe was lost in the street. The wind took away my mitten. The kitty is where the kitty likes to sit. I can see him if I lean and peek. Father says: Sit up. The peas are in the plate. The cake stays in a box. The man says: *Now let's hear from our own Miss Kitty Carlisle with Bless This House.* The bread is white and stacked up. The butter has a little knife. The oven has a window. I can peek inside and see the body sitting in a silver tub. Mother keeps a string tied around and around the body so it can't get out. The tub is on a rack. The oven door makes a scary squeak. The same sound the mouse made when Father found the mouse. I saw it on the bottom-side of his shoe and the shape. We put the body where there were roses and we put a stone to mark the place. Mother puts on the big mitten. Mother pulls out the rack. The body sits very still in the silver tub. It does not try to get out. The tub is full of blood that is browner than blood is. When mud comes in the house it is the color of the blood from the body. When mouths get smacked the blood is the color of the roses that were by the house. When a mouse gets smacked some of it stays on the shoe-bottom. When lambs are tied up the blood is the color of blood. If the string around the body catches fire there are sparks. Then Mother waves a rag. Then Father opens a window. Mary had a little lamb Father says to Sissy when he pokes the big fork in the body and lifts it up and blood leaks from the holes in the side of the body and drips down into the big white plate. Father likes the kind of mustard that is brown with browner specks. Grey PooPoo Father says and looks at me and Sissy and I laugh like he likes me to laugh. Father says Grey PooPoo has more of a kick. Father puts it on the body with a knife. There are pickles sitting in a little dish. Father calls the dish a monkey dish. Father says: That is a dish for a monkey's supper. We don't have a monkey. But we always go to see the monkey when we go to see the man. The monkey is in the back where the curtain is and chained up to the box. The monkey jumps when the man pushes buttons on the box that ring the bell on the box and then the drawer opens up. Sometimes the man says watch and slams and slams the drawer on the box and the bell rings and rings and the monkey jumps and jumps. The chain is short. His hair is all gone on his neck. His teeth stick out. You think he is smiling but he is not. You can see where his foot was hurt. You can see where there is monkey-poo on the paper. You can make a wish on the monkey if you put a penny in his hand. Sometimes the monkey bites if you are not quick. There are pennies in the monkey's monkey dish. There is no dinner in the monkey's monkey dish. There is water in the monkey's cup but there is poo in there too and on the paper. My cup has the Smiling Scotty and he is always smiling on my cup. The salt and pepper men wear big hats. There is soda in my cup. Today is cherry. Tomorrow is orange. Lime is the day there's nothing else left. Sissy does not like lime. I like to put lime in Sissy's cup. Father has to cut her pieces of the body. Father tells me: You are big enough. Mother tips the silver tub and pours the blood into a special pot with a spout. Mother calls the pot for blood a boat. Grandma has a boat for blood in her kitchen. Grandma cuts the body in little bites even if I am old enough. I make a hole in the potatoes with the bottom-side of my spoon. Father holds the blood boat and pours blood into the hole. I can put parts of the body in my mouth myself with no one cutting. I can show Sissy the parts of the body all chewed up in my mouth. Sissy cries and holds her lamb. Father says: Stop or no cake. The cake is in the tied-up box. The string is red and white with knots and Mother hurts her hand when she tries to break the string. Mother said: Stop stop stop it hurts. I peeked in the door. The room was dark but I could hear. The bed made a scary squeak. The door was open enough. Father said: Who's there? Father has the big knife. Father does not like cake. He says: Never liked cake. The cake makes a mark on the side of the box in the shape of a monkey. The monkey has a hurt foot. The cake has a special plate that makes a song and turns all around. Mother lifts up the cake. The roses are the color of the blood. Mother puts the cake on the special plate and turns the winder click click click. We hear the song inside the plate. The cake turns with the song. The candles ride and the fire on the top of each candle moves as if there is a wind inside our house. We sing faster than the plate. Then we are done singing. The song inside the plate tries to catch up. I don't know where to look. Mother lifts a rose off with a knife and puts it on my dish. Mother gives me the knife and says: Make the first cut. I start to push the knife. Father says: Too big. Father puts his hand where the knife is in my hand. He makes the knife go down fast through the cake. Mother dug the roses out. The stone stayed. Mother says: Eat. The man says: *That was our own Miss Kitty Carlisle with Bless This House and thank you Kitty.* The silver tub is cold. The kitty is under the table. He stands on two legs the way he likes to stand. Father says: Get down. The kitty rubs his face along the seat where Father sits. Father says: I said get down. I put the rose into my mouth. Father says: Didn't I say get? and kicks. This house, Father says. This house.

# AS THOSE WHO KNOW
# THE DEAD WILL DO

They went to where there would be canyons, where the daughter had once walked in her younger years, had traveled along the bluffs and ledges, had seen those vast regions of sage and mesa cleft with chasms of stone and the rivers of their incision—and now wanting the father to see—while there was still time, while there was still breath and sense and flow through those most turbulent of tributaries within his fisted heart—wanting the father to see again what he had already seen, though long ago and largely from the air.

"Test flights, training missions," the father said. Runways, he told her, were the desert floor, posts and markers on the hardpan. "Whole days of nothing but sky," he said. "You almost forgot that somewhere there was a war."

The daughter remembered her earlier travels, her somewhat reckless trips of decades past—unaccompanied and unencumbered treks along unmarked trails, scrambling up slants of rock, clambering along switchbacks for a look at flora and fauna—a bird in the mesquite, a cactus in bloom. Such a trip for the two of them—daughter and father—could hardly be considered, considering the father's age, considering what was referred to as his current condition and a conflict of medical opinions: his heart—that was the culprit—or the conduits thereof. There was too much pressure in the vessels, they said, or too little perfusion. Platelets were being under-produced or perhaps they were just sequestered out of place.

Words were constantly flying about: aorta, tricuspid, a man on the brink. Whatever it was, it was slow and steady, a definite disintegration of parts.

"Those big old bombers," the father said. "I'll bet they're still out there on Paradise Field. Not every one was junked for scrap."

"Where exactly?" said the daughter.

"The desert," said the father. "The Southern Mojave. Or maybe it was the Northern Sonora."

"Well, we'd better go see," she said, "before there's nothing left."

She wondered what the world looked like as you left it behind, as it dropped away.

"You go up," the father told her, "and the earth seems to tilt. Heart-stopping," he said. "You'll see."

The daughter did see: how the father went pale with any gain in elevation—half of a city block uphill, a driveway's upward tilt. She saw how he had to stop and pretend to check his watch while hoping for more time.

"Out there, everything's level," the father said, "except for the foothills. No ground references, no depth perception. You pick a place to land," he said, "and you watch the size of your shadow. You make an educated guess."

Years, the daughter guessed. A decade left, hopefully. Time

enough, she decided, for an outing of sorts for the two of them. There was time enough for that, at least.

Though she noticed how he sometimes went sweaty or pale and how walking was in fits and starts. "Wait up," he would say when he lagged behind. "Nothing serious," he said. "Just a little winded."

Breath was short. There were pangs. "Pain?" the daughter asked.

"Not exactly," the father said. "More like a fluttering or wing beat. More like a flap."

Consultations and deliberations ensued. Fibrillations were suspected. Beats were out of rhythm. "Slightly out of whack," the father said.

They wired him up to check conduction: a small box strung over-the-shoulder on a strap.

Contractions were thereby traced in flips and spikes.

The father thought he felt a buzzing in his chest. "Palpitations?" the daughter asked.

"Not exactly," the father said. "More like a run of thumps. More like the hop-skip just before a jump."

Rhythm strips were deciphered. There were abnormal pauses. There were blips and bleeps out of sync.

"Dot-dot-dash," the father said. "All these years, I still remember. Ask me to tap out something besides SOS."

Pills were prescribed to prevent clots, promote pumping, open arteries, assist valves, enhance flow, lower the pressure, increase perfusion. "Quite an assortment," the father said. "How does each pill know where to go?"

The daughter arranged containers and sorted capsules and tablets into plastic boxes with compartments meant to improve compliance. One pill at breakfast, two at dinner; one tab on odd days and one-half on even. The daughter made labels and wrote out instructions with big black markers in big black print.

She shook a bottle that rattled too full. "What about these," she said. "Are these the ones you're taking?"

"Sure," the father said. "Which are those? The little white ones? Sure," he said.

"But are you remembering which and when?" the daughter asked.

"Hell," the father said. "What do you take me for?"

Memory deficits were suggested. The daughter, however, suspected a case of simple devil-may-care.

"Flight patterns, fuel expenditure formulas—it was all up here," he said as he tapped his head, and they had him rewired, retested, rescanned. Carotid flow was sounded for obstruction. Gray matter was imaged for shrinkage.

"See?" the father said, when the final report came in: mentation remains undiminished; capacity for problem solving unimpaired; faculties entirely intact.

"I'm in pretty good shape for the shape I'm in," the father said.

Except for old joints wearing out—the knees that crunched and creaked when flexed. The swelling in an elbow. The hands, when held in extension, that shook.

Something was delicately falling to pieces. "Landing gear fell off," said the father. "Ailerons came hinged, props cracked."

A fender-bender shortly occurred, a mishap in traffic. The father was duly issued a ticket. "The other guy," the father said, "riding in my blind spot. Side-swiped me clear out of the blue."

Impaired night vision, the doctor announced. A problem with rods and cones and clouds in the lens.

"You're coming in for a landing and it's zero visibility," the father said. "Desert wind and dust devils on the runway. Sand in the gears."

Something was slowly grinding to a stop.

Specialists were enlisted.

The daughter kept reports, kept watch, kept appointments. Waiting rooms were cramped.

The wall clocks clicked. Hands were wrung with worry. Footed canes were tapped to the floor, the timing of impatience. Crutches poorly propped in corners slid and clattered. Loose dentures clicked.

Old men dozed, listing into the plastic plants or tilting into tattered magazines, their noses dripping snot. The womenfolk wiped, scolded, surreptitiously tore apart back issues of *Better Homes and Gardens* and *Retirement Living* and pocketed recipes low in sodium and sugar and fat. They flipped through the well-thumbed ads for elevated toilet seats and adaptable baths, and folded the pictures of recreational vehicles into the big purses that sat on their laps. The rip of pages seemed nearly ear-splitting, but among that company few could hear.

A name was called. Half the population stood. "Eh? Come again? Was that my name?" A couple stood, both shaky specimens but sweetly leaning; she with a taped-down tube protruding from a sleeve; he with a transparent bag of urine peeking from a trouser cuff and a wire sticking clavicular.

The father leaned toward the daughter and nodded in their direction. "See that guy?" he whispered in a volume quite easily overheard. "Just shoot me when I get that bad," he said.

Heads turned. "Fine," the daughter said, not looking his way.

"Just turn on the gas," the father said.

"All right," the daughter said.

"Or a little push from a plane," the father said. "Leave the parachute home."

"Shh, will you?" the daughter said.

"Or," the father said, "if there's a plug, go right ahead and pull it. Or use a pillow. Your choice," he told her. "I leave it to you."

"Shut up," the daughter said.

Music intended to be soothing was piped. Voices entered from the vents. The receptionists sat behind a Plexiglas panel, applying polish to their nails and war paint to their faces. Hostilities ran high. Ringing phones were slammed. Buttons flashed in multiples. The panels sometimes slid open and orders were issued: Take a seat. Go on in. Check, cash, or credit card? Expiration date?

Files were handed over. Those of the frailer had more bulk.

Information was dispensed at irregular intervals: Hey, Honey, not too much longer. He's next, Sweetie. You're next, Pop.

"Oooh," said the daughter. "How dare they?"

"What?" the father said.

Exam rooms were cold and sparsely furnished: desk, swivel chair, papered table. "Cold," the father said in his paper gown, now suddenly and overly elderly, seemingly small. The daughter looked when the father was not looking. When had this happened? When was this change, this rapid rate of decline?

"Let me ask you something," the father said. "Which doctor is this?"

The desk held a plastic model of innards in a tangle and a cut-away view of a compromised lung. An artificial artery—over-sized and transected—was clearly impassable, larded up.

Someone in pastels stuck in her head. Ear hoops. Chewing gum. Snap and pop. She proffered a cup, her nails painted the pink of healthy perfusion and embellished with lightning bolts. Her bracelet was bangles, all a-tinkle. "Can you pee?" she said. "Can you spit?"

"Oh, I can spit," the daughter said in tones blatantly inaudible, her head bent low. "Just watch me," she said, and she seethed, steamed under a wall-hung cross section of the human heart, its chambers congested and heart strings stretched.

"Take it easy," the father said. "Just relax. You'll give your self a condition."

The daughter snooped through drawers and unlocked cabinets. Alcohol pads, cotton balls, prescription pads, lab requisitions. What ever might come in handy and was in easy reach.

The father heartily approved of pilferage. "Good," he said. "Go right ahead and steal something. For what they're charging, clean 'em out."

Results came in on clip-boards, in folders, in the pockets of white cotton coats and accompanied by smiles, by so-how-are-yous and then the more serious tones and layman's terms: contractions were inadequate; valves were leaking.

"Those early engines, at the start of the war," the father said.

Corpuscles were lacking carrying capacity.

"Fuel pumps breaking down," the father said. "Radio failures."

Multiple pieces were pumping out of sequence.

"Crankshaft troubles," the father said. "Machine gun freeze-ups."

Spark plugs, crankshafts, coronary arteries.

"Lucky we had good ground crews," the father said. "Lucky we had spare parts."

A valve was evidently in need of replacement. Possibly two.

"When?" the daughter said.

Who can say? they said. It all hinged on circumstances. It would depend on surgical risks and risk-benefit ratios. Response—or not—to blood thinners and thickeners. Conclusions, however, indicated that there were occlusions. Would a gasket hold? Would a splice be enough? Blood was tail-spinning down a vessel. Something supposed to be ascending was taking a nose-dive to somewhere else.

"Surgical intervention," the doctors told them. "Strongly suggested" was the wording.

"Hold on," the father said. "What's the rush?"

"Don't hold off," they said, "or you'll be too far gone."


They went to where there would be mesas, where there would be mountain passes and expanses of sky. Plans had been hastily made. The daughter, knowing the lay of the land, laid out alternate routes, ways of going with walking at a minimum—strolls only, she told the father. A matter of merely a few steps from the car to selected scenic lookouts and back. Door to door. Canyon to canyon. And possibly, if he were up to it, a leisurely amble along a path or two without incline.

Did he think it would be more than he could handle? she asked the father. More than he could do?

"You heard the man," the father said. "I'm not dead yet."

"All right then," she said—It would be a motor trip primarily, to places the father might remember, places now only hinted at on the map: restricted area, former airfield, impassable road. By now, military posts were most likely ghost towns; abandoned barracks might not be standing; old runways, she supposed, were long ago overgrown.

"There's still some old bombers out there, turning to rust," the father said. "It will be the last time I'll sit in a cockpit."

No time like the present, the daughter said. They would drive. They would have their maps and navigate. They would find their way just fine, make stops at diners and snack bars wherever. Find motels in the middle of nowhere.

A last chance, she told him, to see what was left of the West.


They went to where there the roads are open—where the byways are two-lanes lightly traveled. Where distances are deceptive.

Scenery rushes by, a landscape of sameness. The daughter at the wheel, pointing out points of interest. The father, a passenger, reading the map.

"Shotgun," says the daughter.

"Navigator, you mean," the father says.

He notes the cloud formations over elevated ranges, or the lack thereof in the unrelenting blue; he spots the roadside shrines that mark crack-ups and crashes: the wooden markers held by piles of stones, the crepe flowers faded by desert weather.

She sights birds: raptors and roadrunners; there a red-tail on a pole, a cactus wren in a thicket; and that speck, that high-up mote—she points: a buzzard riding currents off a ridge, sailing on the heat.

The asphalt seems to waver.

The cerulean sky close to the horizon fades to bone, to burning white above.

Clouds are sparse, their shadows curving, conforming to the foothill shapes. A distant lake is a shimmer of distortion, draining as they approach. They pick up speed. What looks like a rabbit is a stick. What looks like a stick is a toad. A toad near the shoulder is a stone.

"The desert air plays tricks," she says.

"Always did," the father says.

The radio plays country-western.

"How can you listen to this crap?" the father says, then turns the volume up.

"This road," he says, "looks familiar."

"How could you know?" she says.

Well, he says, there was the one time—he tells her—when he traveled these parts not airborne, but on terra firma. One time for a pal of his, he says, a fellow cadet. It was a training flight, a routine up and down, and he tells her how he stood watching from the airstrip, looking up, seeing the fire in the fuselage, the black smoke spiraling, the tail breaking away, and finally the parachute not forthcoming. How quickly it went down, he remembers, and how the pieces of the desert—rock, dust, rock—rose up. How he—her father—made his way by bus to the dusty town where the boy was born, where the mother and the father of the boy sat at the kitchen table as those who know the dead have always done, as those who know the dead will do—will always do—and there in the kitchen the mother of the dead boy gave her father coffee and a slice of pie—cherry, he remembers, or maybe persimmon. How the father of the boy—of the dead boy—sat sitting with them so silent in the kitchen, not saying a word until it was time, and then it was time, and the father of the boy finally speaking and saying to her father, to the stranger in their kitchen, the visitor: You were the only one come on out all this way, the only one who knew my boy.

A pal of mine, the father says. Or sort of a pal, the father says. Not exactly a pal, but someone from flight school. Paradise Field, out here. These parts. Or maybe it was Texas. The part they call the panhandle, or somewhere there.

And well, not exactly a pal, the father tells the daughter. Just someone I met once or maybe twice, he says, or hitched out with on leave, or sat next to at mess.

They drive on. Attempts are made to stay on schedule. The daughter has taken into account distances, hours of daylight, the necessity for rests. They pull over in the shade of a boulder—other shade nowhere to be had—to unwrap sandwiches and drink their bottled water. They stop for leg-stretching at turnouts and peer over overlooks. They stop at the spots marked "Scenic View."

At a truck stop store she buys a jam made from the fruit of the prickly pear. He buys a felt hat, the cowboy kind.

"Stetson?" the daughter says when they are back on the road.

"Not exactly," the father says, checking under the brim. "Made in Taiwan," he says. "Imported crap."

The day grows later. They drive on.

Tonight's lodging is still a little ways away. "Somewhere up ahead," she says, just a town or two. Not far, according to the father, according to the map.

"In time for dinner," the daughter says.

The rocks take on the color of the sunset. The evening air still holds the gusts of afternoon heat.

They roll down the windows and smell the sage. The dry earth. The salt of old oceans.

The sky becomes a darker shade. Now the passing bluffs in shadow with shadowy clefts and the shelves of stone shaped by the force of long-spent rivers. The sun nearly down, but the world still undark with the spill of light lower than the horizon.

They are speeding now, the father and the daughter. They are putting miles behind them, hoping to make time.

The mesas now stand in silhouette. Clouds clump above the cooling desert floor, blue-bottomed, almost unmoving. "Slow wind, out of the west," the father says, observing drift.

Up ahead, dead vegetation bounces across the road. There are little twisters of dust where the road is seen to split—asphalt straight ahead and a turnoff to the left.

She stops now, beside the unpaved way lined with leaning wood-posts strung with old barbed wire in broken skeins.

"Here," the father says, folding away the map.

"This?" the daughter says.

"Yes," the father says. "The old runway. Now I remember. The back way in to Paradise Field."

"I don't know about that," the daughter says.

A sign hangs at a slant by a single nail. Bits of paint still cling, but just enough: No Tres. Keep Out.

"Yes," he says. "This is it. It's all coming back."

"All right," the daughter says.

They turn in. The way is all ruts and dips, edged with dry mesquite and broken spears of stone. They bump along in the dust. Jolt and thump. They swerve away from rock shards that stick up enough to split an oil pan, sharp enough to slice a tread.

"Have we got a spare?" the daughter says.

"Spare what?" the father says.

They drive on.

The road ends in rubble. A rockslide blocks. They stop. The engine cools and ticks. The sweet air. The dry wind. The blooming cactus pear.

"Come on," he says, pushing the car door open with his foot. "Help me up."

A trace of a trail leads through the brush, the path being one a small animal might travel. The way is nearly level here, the ground dry and beaten. "This way," the father says, already ahead, tottering on.

A fence still stands—chain linked and leaning, a mesh of sags and gaps. There is no entranceway or gate. A cotton-wood, lightning split, presses heavily where one might easily step.

"We shouldn't," the daughter says.

"I flew the damn things, didn't I?" the father says.

"Someone might come," the daughter says.

"No one is," the father says.

The sun has decidedly set. The path is dim but for the whiteness of the hardpan in the final light. "Careful," the daughter says.

A form beyond, some ways away, largely looms. "There," he says. "There it is."

"What?" the daughter says.

"The last old bomber—I knew we'd find it," says the father. "I knew there'd be at least one left."

Shapes are not easily discerned. Pale stones and evening primrose seem to glow. A shred of feathers in a brittlebush hangs ghostly.

Already there are early stars.

Something scurries in the underbrush. Overhead is a fluttering, a series of hoots.

The path becomes a slight incline. Crunch of rock under their feet. Small stones roll. The father stumbles. "Watch out," the daughter says. "Maybe we'd better not."

The father heaves a breath. "A little uphill," he says and starts again, tremulous this time and clutching at a smoke-tree stem.

"Pain?" the daughter says.

"No," the father says. "Just the old ticker."

There are more steps to take, with brush along the way and clumps of sage to navigate. "Here," she says, and takes him by the arm. "Hold on."

The form ahead of them emerges in the gloom. "There," the father says. "See it?"

She bends a slender bough away.

There. Yes. Now she does. She sees. The bulk of it beyond a weedy stand of salt cedar, left here long ago in what must be a clearing: the shape of hulking fuselage, the broken tail, and there—that must be the wing.

They step into the shadow of it. They lean in through the weedy stand of cedar.

But there is no smooth hull of sheeted steel still hot with the heat left by the desert day; no flaking sides of peeling paint that crumble to the touch. This dark-shaped thing is rough—rough to the knuckle, scraping their fingers—and it is solid and cold—not steel at all, but stone. A boulder, one in a row of boulders—nothing more than that—along a ridge where father and daughter now stand, high up.

"Careful," the daughter says. "There's a drop."

And now the clearing opens onto overhang and edge. Father and daughter, daughter and father: they peer out on the empty stretch of desert, on those vast and distant territories lit by the spill of stars and bordered by the insubstantial line where the land meets sky, sky meets land.

Where the curvature of earth gives way to its turning and seems to slide away from the place where they stand with their backs to the great cold stone, and where the view is of the empty space beyond the precipice.

# ARROW CANYON

Out here where we are, down this end of the county, we don't have much in the way of attractions. Not any more, anyways. Unless you'd call the Ute jerky stand an attraction. Or even Arrow Canyon—that used to bring folks in. Used to be you could get yourself up in one of those little rock shelters and haul out all sorts of crap. What they call artifacts—those things the ones they call The Old Ones made: carvings and whatnot, clay pots and such. There's nothing left of course. Looters had it pretty much cleaned out by the time Indian Affairs got wind of it. Now there's not so much as a shard. But Arrow Canyon—sure. That used to be a draw. So was the rodeo, when it was. Three towns west, and we always got the overflow. But it's a dozen years—at least—since the rodeo closed after that rope thing with the boy, that Murdock boy. Since then there's not much else to bring folks in. Sure, we get a few locals, but mostly it's your truckers, your salesmen, the odd motorist who winds up here by accident—everybody on their way to somewheres else. So no wonder I notice these three—the ones checked into Unit 4—when I'm pushing the cart past the office and Hank pokes his head out and says: Luce, how's the count?

How's the count is what Hank always says when he sees me headed for more towels—hand, face, and bath—which is what he is asking about—and I tell him: Good Hank, the count's good. That's what I always say. But the actual count? As in: Am I keeping track of who tucked what into which suitcase and hightailed it down the interstate? Forget it. Cups yes—the ceramic ones for the Mister Coffee. Or sort of yes. You'd wonder who'd want a cup with a cactus in a cowboy hat, but like they say: There's no accounting. So cups—the ceramic ones—sure. But your plastic-wrapped tumblers? Your hot-or-cold containers? No. I don't think so.

And not the single-use soaps either, not that he's asking. He's a stickler, that Hank, when he gets to do his management thing, which is how he gets now and then. But it passes. With six units and one adjoining, and what Hank calls a limited staff—which is limited to it being just me—you cut corners, no matter what Hanks says. The johns for instance. If there's nothing really that obvious—and let me spare you the gory details—all they get is a spritz of Clean-Latrine and that Sanitized-For-Your-Protection strip goes on. Sanitized. That's a good one.

Hey. We're not La Quinta. We're not the Ramada Inn.

As for cups, Hank caught on to the count being off pretty fast when Unit 4 called the office: Can we get cups in here?

So now here's Hank inquiring about cactus cups, as in where are they, and not when I'm out wrapping up the 11 AM check-outs either. No, Hank is asking at 11 in the PM, and at that hour when someone comes around unannounced and asking as to where the cups in 4 got to, let me tell you: It's a bit of a jolt when you're in for the night, in bed for the night with your hot cup of something, such as your cup-of-soup or your instant what-have-you that you fixed with your portable immersible that Hank says don't use, it will flip the circuit breakers but anyway you do, you always do and somehow it never does, and Hank comes a-rapping. Luce? he says. You in there?

Am I in there. Am I in there. That's a good one. Where else would I be?

What? I yell back.

What happened to the cups in 4? he says.

What happened? What does he think happened? Gone is what. Packed up, wrapped up—probably in one of the hand-size towels—and gone. If it's a guest-room amenity, it'll walk. Ice buckets, lotion, soap. You name it. Even the complimentary coffee slash sweetener slash non-dairy creamer packs. Or the entire condiment presentation caddy and the in-room copy of Fun In & Around Canyon Country. Someone once walked off with the gratuity envelope. You know: We Hope You Enjoyed Your Stay! Come Again Soon! Your Housekeeper has been _____. Like they say: If it ain't nailed down. They'd take the Mister Coffee if the carafe would fit in a suitcase. They'd take the clock radio if it wasn't such a piece of crap.

Luce, he says. You up? Luce? and raps some more.

I know he's not going away, that Hank.

So I throw off my covers and head for the door. I keep the chain on, as if I need some privacy, as if Hank's not allowed in, though he's been in. Plenty of times. Times too numerous to mention. But tonight, no. I'm just not up for it even if he is, so to speak.

What's this now? I say as if I didn't hear him.

He leans in as close as he can with his mouth near the chain. Luce, he says real low. Sorry to get you up this late but where are you keeping the cups? Just tell me, he says. Don't get up.

Don't get up.

But I am, and the last thing I want is Hank messing around in the supply closet and messing it up and/or finding things. Or not finding things.

What unit? I ask him.

Three cups for Unit 4, he says. But Luce, he says. I can get them. Just tell me where.

Go back to bed Hank, I tell him.

You sure Luce? he says. You sure?

I wait until I hear Hank shut the office door so I know the coast is clear and I go out.

I stand a while. It's a clear night. Sound travels.

The generator over at the Murdock place revs up and starts to hum the way it does when their power goes out. And it's always going out, out their way, just off the grid. It's straight-out flat and nothing but sage, so you can just about see their place from here, especially if you're standing on the dumpster. Not that there's much to see. Used to be they had a regular working ranch out there—nothing big, mind you, but they did all right—Johnny and his daddy and his ma. Twenty acres it was, or maybe twenty-five, and cattle mainly but some wool-sheep, too. But that's gone. Been gone. Sold off. Now it's just the house sitting on a little plot. Not much to see.

I stand a while more. There's stars. There's moon. The wind comes up.

There's the smell of mesquite from the Ute fire and the smell of sage—there's always that—and then there's the smell of whatever's blooming out there this time of year.

Cliff-rose maybe.

For a second I re-think that Hank thing, but it passes. A yip-yip from somewhere in the dark brings me around.

It's that coyote I've been seeing—a raggedy old boy nosing around the Murdock place and once out by our dumpster. Yip-yipping all by his lonesome.

Damn that Hank.

Over at the Murdock's, the generator rumbles off as the power kicks in. A light goes on in their kitchen: Johnny's ma, I'll bet, fixing him some dinner. And in the backroom—the back bedroom—that'd be his daddy emptying the bucket they keep by his bed. They're getting on in their years, Mr. and Mrs. Murdock—in their sixties by now. At least.

I take the cart—the whole shebang. There's always someone who will hear me rumbling by and ask for an extra who-knows-what. Toilet paper, tissues, lotion, soap. But it's light tonight with three units vacant, three units filled, and two of them are regulars so to speak. There's Mendez in 5, from over at the U-Totem since his wife threw him out. There's a couple in 6 whose names I won't mention but one of which wouldn't want anyone spotting his pickup parked in plain view in her drive, if you get my drift. And then there's those folks in 4.

We get just the one station—Country Ten-Seven—and they've got it on in there, in 4. Reception is better at night most nights, unless we've got rain coming. I don't know why that is. Hank says sunspots, but then Hank says lots of things.

But tonight it's clear and starry, and the music's coming through just fine. And not to be nosey, but they've got the lights on and the drapes open so I can see right in and you can bet I've seen just about everything there is to see when the drapes are open like that. Just about everything, and then some. So I'm passing by the big window, not turning my head to look since that would be too obvious and what do I see with those drapes open but two of them in there up and dancing.

And these two, they're no kids either—the two of them that's dancing—and neither is the oldest one, an old grey-haired guy sitting in a chair. I could see that when they checked in—the three of them. The two cutting the rug I figured to be a couple, and the other one I took to be the daddy—her dad-dy—since I hear her say: I'll get that Daddy—when the daddy is lugging in his stuff and looking pretty shaky, breathing hard and looking just about done in.

I give a little knock. I say what I say: Housekeeping.

Hold on, she says through the door. Turn that down, she says.

The radio goes low and she opens up.

You folks need cups? I say.

Oh yes, she says. Come on in.

Right away I can see they're a pretty messy bunch, these three. They've got newspapers spread all around and maps un-folded, and the suitcases open on the bed and the floor with all sorts of clothes hanging out.

And on the floor around the old guy in the chair—the dad-dy—there's crumpled-up tissues where he missed the trashcan.

Not that you could fit anything else in the trashcan. It's already filled up with paper cups and empty pop bottles and banana peels and what looks like the wrappings of those Ready-Wrap sandwiches that Mendez sells over at the U-Totem.

She takes the cups and sets them by the Mister Coffee. Joe, she says, give me a few bucks.

Oh that's not necessary, I say—which is what you say. But thank you anyways.

No no, she says. We must have gotten you out of bed, she says. Joe, she says: Give me a five.

She's making me dance, Joe says reaching in his pocket.

Not me, says the daddy.

You're next Daddy, she says.

They've got the bathroom lights on—both the overhead and the sink—so it's easy to see that it's already mussed up in there, too. The shower curtain is half in, half out—which, by the way, drives Hank to distraction. They've got towels hung half-assed on the edge of the tub and the curtain rod, and the bathmat's all rumpled.

You folks need anything else? I say. More towels maybe? A few more soaps?

I think we're OK, she says.

Let me get you some extra towels at least, I tell her. Looks like you could use a few, I say and give a little nod toward the bathroom. Hey, I'm thinking: there's a big load of laundry coming my way anyways, so what's a few more? And with that tip, the five?

Cart's right outside, I tell them. It will only take a minute.

Well, she says.

And I pop out and load up: three fresh hand towels, three face, three bath; a brandy-new box of Kleenex, a bunch of hand-and-body lotion combo packs, a bunch of single-use soaps. Why not? I mean: the five. Who gives you a five?

In the bathroom, it's a real mess. Worse than I thought. Toothpaste squishing out of the tube. Whiskers in the sink. Hair on a comb. Pee drips on the seat. That kind of thing. And there's some kind of machine plugged in, some kind of thing with a hose on it and a little jar of water attached. Something for breathing into, I think. Or breathing out of. Plus there's bunch of medicine bottles on the toilet tank, and a plastic see-through box full of pills set inside little squared-off spaces marked Morning and Evening. For the old guy, I figure. The real old guy—the daddy. No wonder he's looking like he looks.

I fix the shower curtain. I put the damp towels on the rack. I wipe out the sink. I wipe off the seat. I flush the toilet and put down the lid and put the new stuff on top, arranged real nice.

I turn off the bathroom light. OK, I say. You're all set.

Well thanks, she says.

You all have a good night, I tell them.

But the old guy, the daddy—he stops me: Hold on Miss, he says. You live around here?

She won't know, the woman says.

Sure she will, the old daddy tells her. Go on, show her that map, that place we're looking for, he says. What's it called? he says. Arrow Canyon?

It's that crappy map that Ed Little Bird hands out at the Ute jerky stand. Drew it himself, I happen to know. He's got those big-arm cactus stuck in here and there, even though there's none of those anywhere around these parts—except the ones on the coffee cups—and a road-runner running at the bottom of the page, which I have seen smashed flat out on ninety-seven. He's got the reservation boundary all marked off with teepees which the Utes don't have and never did, and a big stick of jerky marked You Are Here which looks pretty right to me. And he's got a dotted line for the dirt road into Arrow Canyon.

Well Miss? says the daddy.

I've got the map in my hand. I move in closer to the light by the bed.

It's not to scale, I say, but the turnoffs are right. Except that left off ninety-seven can be a little tricky. It's a lot closer than it looks.

I look at the three of them and they're all looking at the map and nodding. The Joe guy is rubbing his chin.

See? says the daddy. What did I tell you? I told you she'd know. Like I always say: Just ask the locals.

What do you want with Arrow Canyon? I say.

Well, she says, I thought we'd have a look at the petroglyphs.

Petroglyphs?

The carvings and the rock art, she says.

The rock art. So right away I think that maybe they're thinking there's still stuff to steal out there. Not that the old guy, the daddy, is doing any climbing up rocks. Hey. He barely made it in the door with the luggage.

No point in going on out there, I say. Everything's cleared out, out there.

Cleared out? she says.

Looters, tourists, I tell her. There's no pots anymore, I say. Everything's long gone.

Not pots, she says. Just what's on the rocks. We heard there's carvings on the rocks and on the canyon walls. Symbols, she says. Hunting scenes.

Who says? I say.

The Ute, Joe says. The one who gave us the map.

The Ute. Right. Ed Little Bird. I look at that map one more time and I see where he's got a little deer drawn in and a stick figure of a hunter with a bow. Like something a kid might do.

Sure, I tell her. There's all kinds of scratching on the rocks. That rock art I mean. But you can't get those rocks out, I tell her. You can't just hike in there and pick them up. Everything's too big for you all to be hauling out without a truck. Or a backhoe, even. It's nothing you can just pick up and put in your pocket. It's all on the cliffs and the boulders, I tell her.

We're not collecting, Joe says. We just want to take a look, he says. We drive to places to take a look. It's why we came out here, he says.

Just to look?

We're not interested in taking anything out, she says.

Just to look. Now this is just amazing. These three out here not just by accident, but coming out here, coming all this way—and who knows where they're coming from—just to be looking at scribbles—at scratches—on a rock. Amazing.

She drags me all over, Joe says.

Me too, says the daddy, and he starts getting up from the chair, or trying to. He makes what looks like a big effort to push himself up—grunting and such—but he flops back down.

Here you go Daddy, she says, and she puts her arm under his. On three. Up you go.

Now this old guy is pretty wobbly, but he pushes her off. Just wait, will you? he says. Just give me a minute. And he rocks back and forth some and then he's up on his own.

Well look at that, she says. Much better, she says.

Horse shit, says the daddy.

My father here—he's having a little trouble walking these days, she says.

Oh hell, the daddy says, I can make it. I made it this far.

Can we see them—the carvings—from the road? says Joe. I'm not so big on hiking around in the heat myself.

Oh you two, she says to the two of them.

Sure, I say. You can see them. And it shouldn't be too hot if you get an early start. Not this time of year.

Would we need a guide? she says. The Ute—he offered to take us out there but I thought we'd try it ourselves.

And now I'm thinking: Well wouldn't that Ed Little Bird be more than happy to show them around? Rock art. Right. He probably snuck out there and chipped in a few new ones himself. Just to make it more interesting.

You don't need a guide, I tell her. Just cut off ninety-seven right where the road splits, I say and I show them on the map. You head on through a little wash, I tell her, and it's all over the place, the rock art. On the big boulders. On the canyon walls. All kinds of carvings and marks and symbols and such. You can see them from the road. Just go slow. Keep looking up.

See, says the daddy. She knows. What did I tell you?

Just watch that first turnoff, I say.

OK, she says. Will do. Come on Daddy, she says. Time for bed.

Hold on a minute, the old guy says. Miss, he says to me. One more thing: Any place around here where we can get a few beers?

It's late now. There's no wind, but it's colder. And quiet. Even that old coyote must have turned in. Except there's a light still on over at the Murdock's place. There is every night. There's all kinds of chores they've got to do before getting Johnny ready for bed. The bed, the bucket. The food that gets mashed up. There's a tube and the mashed-up food goes in the tube and there's a special way you hold it up. Mrs. Murdock showed me. She showed me that and she showed me other things. How the other tube comes out. How his breathing thing goes on. How his arms and legs should go.

~

I hear them leaving in Unit 4 early, before the sun is up. Getting an early start before the heat. There's the usual banging around folks do when they're checking out. I lean over the end of my bed and peek out through the curtain. She's out there. She's leaning against the car with her elbows on the roof. She's got her binoculars out, looking off in the direction of the Murdock place.

What's she looking out there for? I'm thinking.

Joe! she says in the kind of a whisper you could hear three doors down.

I hear him just a little ways off, behind the screen door.

What? he says. What is it?

Shh! she says, waving him over, starting to hand him off the binoculars. Coyote, she says. Take a look. And he comes on out and lets that screen door slam shut behind him.

Joe! she says.

*Where?* Joe says. *Where is he?*

*Well, nowhere now! You scared him off!* He was over there, right by that house with his head in the garbage.

*You sure it wasn't a dog?* he says.

*It was a coyote,* she says. *An actual coyote.* But he's gone now. *Jeez Joe,* she says.

~

I'm heading down the walk with the cart, wrapping up the check-outs, only there's not that much to wrap up this particular morning. Three units. That's all. Mendez, who probably will be back tonight if he didn't patch things up with his wife, and those two from town who probably won't.

And those three, of course. The folks in 4.

I figure they're there by now. The sun's been up a while but even so, it'll be tolerable in Arrow Canyon. This time of year, it's cool enough till noon. And the cliff-rose might be blooming. Might be. Should be. All along the west slope, I remember; there was plenty.

We'd go on out there—out to Arrow Canyon—me and Johnny Murdock. We used to go around together for a while, though mostly he was busy with his daddy's ranch, the twenty or so acres. And he'd make a little extra when the rodeo came through, setting up barrels and concessions, riding and roping. That sort of thing. And then we'd head out to Arrow Canyon—sometimes when the cliff-rose was blooming and sometimes when it wasn't, and other times just looking for stuff to steal, just like everyone else. Hunting that stuff The Old Ones left behind when they packed up and went wherever they went. Most everything had been carted out by then. Picked clean. The stone shelters under the cliff overhangs all kicked in. But that boy—that Johnny Murdock—he climbed way up in this little space in the rocks. Some little spot high up enough where no one else could get to. That's just how he was—always taking chances, getting into something, doing what he shouldn't. And I'm looking up and shouting for him to be careful and watch out and Johnny, Johnny, come on down! But he's up there a while, past where I can see, and then I hear him: Luce! and he's standing way up there and waving. Waving something. And then he's starting down the slope, nearly running, nearly tumbling, rocks rolling and spilling all around him and he's not even paying no mind and then he's down, he's here all smiling and dusty with that red canyon dirt.

It was a little dog he brought me down. A stone-carved dog the same color as the canyon. An artifact.

I've got it still, that stone dog. Somewheres. I know I do.

They've left the door ajar in Unit 4. It's not such a mess. Not like it was. They've got the trash bagged up and the newspapers stacked and the damp towels in one neat heap. And nothing's missing, either. Not a thing. Six bath towels, six face, six hand. One ice bucket. One clock radio. One Mister Coffee, carafe, and condiment convenience caddy. Three cactus cups.

I check the envelope. You know: We Hope You Enjoyed blah blah. Your Housekeeper has been _____. And hey: There's a five. Another one.

A five. Well.

Hank catches me at the cart. So? Hank says. Everybody checked out?

Sure, I tell him. Everybody's gone.

What time did Mendez leave? he says.

I don't know. Early, probably.

And those two in 5? he says.

Checked out, I tell him, even though he already knows it since the pick-up's gone with them sure in it.

They leave the key? he says.

Yep, I say.

How's the count, Hank says.

As in towels—as in hand, face, and—well, you know.

Good, Hank. Count's good, I tell him.

Good, Luce. Good, he says, and he gives me a thumbs-up and a little wink. So Luce, he says. See you later?

Later, when the beds and bathrooms get done, maybe I'll take a little ride. Hank won't care a whit, just as long as the rooms are ready. Hey, he'll hardly notice.

It's a nice ride. And not too far. You just have to watch for that first turnoff of ninety-seven. It's easy to miss.

The air is sweet out there if the cliff-rose is blooming. And even if it isn't, there's always the smell of sage. Always the sage. There's always that.

# IRREGULARS

He was still working all the while his heart was going bad, still running the business—a garment business of sorts—but it was nothing glamorous, nothing trendy or chic. No, this was the business of buying up dry goods for next to nothing—big batches of damaged stuff—then selling it off dirt cheap—an enterprise he had started with two partners soon after the war, two buddies from the same squadron, who—in short order—turned out to be loafers and spongers—useless early on. But they were long dead by the time everything began to unravel. That last year, that's when I asked him: Was he making any money? Was he in the black or in the red? Bleeding, the old man said, but just a trickle.

He moved it all yearly, all over town—the entire operation: the beat-up office furniture, the stock, the old Singer sewing machines, even the Spanish ladies who did the sewing. Warehouse to warehouse he went, each place a little cheaper, a little smaller, a little shabbier. He dodged the taxman and left no forwarding address.

But he kept at it—dipping into his pension for expenses and putting off paying accounts overdue. Still waking early and heading out to what he called "the office"—the last place—a hanger-sized space in a building of old brick and windows of chicken-wire glass, on the outskirts of the city—a district of bankruptcy and dereliction. There he bought factory seconds and irregulars for a song, taking on whole job-lots in need of repair by the two Spanish ladies. They sat at the old industrial Singers that chirped as the handwheels turned, clicked as the needles dipped. They stitched and restitched, letting down hems or hiking them higher. They cut out the bad parts and replaced mistakes—the stretched-out waistbands, the raggedy cuffs. The whole place smelled of ozone from the spin of the motors, and of *arroz con pollo* and *habichuelas* from the little room out back: *la cocina*, where the Spanish ladies set their pots to boil on the hot plate and made due with a mini-fridge and a single-spouted sink. There was a toilet back there, too, and a cot where the deaf man—Jorge—was allowed to sleep.

Jorge had ridden up in the freight elevator one day, looking for work—or perhaps just a place to sleep—and making the little yelps the deaf will sometimes do. He hooted, he pointed, he danced his wiry self all around. Irk, he said, pretending to hammer. Irk, he said, pretending to sweep. The old man took him on, took him in, and let him live in a corner of the kitchen. There Jorge made his bed—keeping his blankets neatly folded and his bottles of Bacardi largely out of sight. He ate what the Spanish ladies fed him. He ran the freight elevator. He packed orders for delivery and sorted the unsalvageables. He lugged boxes and ran errands. He swept up.

The old man sat in his creaky swivel chair at a dented-up metal desk with his rolodex, telephone, and big old Smith

Corona electric—that's all it took—surrounded by the big strapped-up bales bursting with damaged goods—the trousers with faulty zippers or snaps, the shirts with snags or tears or runs or pulls or armholes sewn shut. He bought and sold over the phone, taking orders and narrowly turning a profit—pennies on the dollar—but a profit nonetheless. Alchemy, he called it—turning crap into gold—he liked to say. The bobbins spun and the Spanish ladies stitched and snipped and ripped, tearing at faulty seams, taking in and letting out. There was always a haze of dust in the air. The old planked floors were strewn with bits of thread and scraps of fabric as the Spanish ladies pushed the cloth along with their fingers and toed the electric treadles, and as the cottony fill from busted-out padded brassieres stirred and drifted cloudlike around the sewers' feet.

He kept on, the old man did. When he was too weak to climb the stairs, Jorge pulled him—and towards the end, carried him up. When the building was condemned and the city shut off the electric, he saw it as a money-saving measure, a reason not to pay rent. But without power, the freight elevator wouldn't work. Goods had to be hauled up through a broken window. The building went cold and dark. Jorge rigged in electric with a wire he ran out to a utility pole, so there was light but no heat. Little indoor clouds hovered and dispersed—the misty exhalations of conversations that came and went. And the old man? He took to wearing an overcoat and an old hunting cap, and long underwear in the very coldest weather. Jorge wrapped himself in his blankets. Jorge drank more rum. But the Spanish ladies—accustomed to warmer climes—filled their pocketbooks with threads and bobbins, and gathered up their pots and left.

The roof began to leak. Rain came through the broken windows. Bales of goods slowly disintegrated. Mice nested in the cartons of cotton briefs and the water-stained stacks of Fruit-of-the-Loom. Mold grew on the bolts of fabric. The old man sat at his desk as boxes of pajamas awaiting shipment bulged and split. To hell with the stock, he finally said. Who needs it?—he said—and he kept on, on the phone. He bought what sat in someone else's warehouse; he sold off his invisible inventory.

When he called—when he finally called—he told me that the building was scheduled for demolition. When? I asked. How much time do you have to get everything out? Well, he said, he could see the crane from the window. Crane? I said. What crane? I asked him. He said: The one attached to the wrecking ball, that's what. When I arrived, a giant dumpster was already stationed at a doorway. Piles of fallen bricks lay in the street.

So we started in, packing up. We packed up "the books"—a shopping bag full of notes and numbers on scraps, on memo pads, on paper napkins. We packed up the phone, the rolodex, the big Smith Corona—all it would take, he said, to keep the business running. He'd start somewhere else, he said—a new place, maybe something smaller. He'd done it plenty times before. He could run it all from home, he said—from his apartment, if he had to. He'd get it all going again—everything up and running—as soon as he'd get back on his feet.

We looked around for Jorge to say goodbye and to give him—as the old man put it, "a few bucks." Jorge's pile of blankets were still in the empty kitchen, and there was piss in an empty rum bottle—the plumbing had been pulled out by vandals—but Jorge was nowhere to be found. Jorge? we called down the dark stairwell. Jorge? we shouted into the shaft of the stuck elevator. But it was only our voices that came back to us—Jorge, Jorge, Jorge—ever fainter and farther away. We called out the window and down into the alley and up through the hole in the roof. Jorge? we shouted, calling the name of deaf man. Jorge.

And so we walked out—out through the remains of it, the wreck of it—stepping over the broken glass from broken windows, the papers scattered all around: yellowing invoices, unpaid bills. A wisp of cottony fluff stuck to the old man's trouser cuffs. A book of swatches lay in a puddle of roof-water—or was it rain? I turned and looked back—I'm not sure if he did, too, or if he didn't. But I looked back and saw the marks on the wide-planked floor where the old sewing machines had once been bolted—now gone—ripped out and sold off. I looked back and I saw the footprints of the old man—the traces of where he was and where he was going—where he had walked through the powdery bits of plaster that were falling as the ceiling was cracking and the walls were crumbling and the place was turning to dust.

# SOMEWHERE IN THE NORTH ATLANTIC

The big woman sleeps and sprawls full out, her bulk unleashed upon the king-sized bed, having room enough for
two. Her nylon nightie clings to her sweating immensity: the
puckered thighs, the heft of rump. She shifts her thick limbs.
The bed frame sags. Posts lean and bed slats ever-so-slightly
bow. Bolts work loose and screws destabilize unseen, unwinding thread by thread, slower than a glacial melt. Her bed is
a freighter, a breaker of ice, bearing her through dreams in
northern waters. The room is cool. She keeps the window
raised an inch or so, even on wintry evenings when the radiator
hisses. The big woman needs no covers, no protection from the
weathers, no external heat. She lies atop the paisley-patterned
spread previously kept plastic-wrapped and hidden away on a
closet shelf, safe from the spills and sweats and smells of the old
man formerly her bedmate but now relegated to a rented bed
a room away, his nighttime misadventures no longer a threat.
He sleeps railed in, newly alone with a view of the river and
the cliffs where trees sprout from cracks in the mighty slants of
rock, and live on nothing and still live.

The daughter—unmarried and middle-aged—sleeps most nights alone in her single-sized bed, having headed for home after feeding the father his dinner as he sat propped up in his rented bed, having provided the father with a bath of sorts—a quick going-over is what she called it, with basin and washcloth and a mild liquid soap and a lukewarm rinse; having applied a lotion with attention to the parts of him most prone to wearing out, wearing thin; having pulled the under-sheet tight and smoothing it free of wrinkles; having placed the disposable pad in its proper position; having pulled the top-sheet and blanket up around his shoulders, and having provided the big woman with revised instructions, with written directions, review of medications, provisions, precautions, contingencies, names, numbers, emergency measures, dietary selections, scenarios and lists; and having bid a goodnight to both the father and the big woman, muttered all manner of unrepeatable oaths to herself once out the apartment door and during her elevator ride down to the parking level. And having arrived home at last to her partially unhinged back door, had gone to her bed still clothed under an unwashed comforter showing shreds of stuffing and clumped with the hair of two cats who daily claw the upholstery unchecked.

The big woman sleeps alone in her king-sized bed, except for the company of foil-wrapped caramels kept under her pillow, and a pack of Hi Ho Crackers and a nice wedge of cheddar positioned on a platter in easy reach. The room is dim. A digital clock gives light enough so that items on the dressing table seem to glow: glass boxes of rings and bangles, bottles of perfume displayed on a mirrored tray, jars of creams for smoothing wrinkles and eradicating age spots, potpourri in a crystal dish.

The father sleeps alone in his rented bed, except for the metal pan for pooping in and the handled jar for pissing in; except for a box of wipes for wiping and a clappered bell for summoning help; except for the current company of the navigator out front and the top turret gunner at the headboard, and the ball turret gunner snugly set below the bedsprings, and the waist gunners waiting on the left and the right, and the tail gunner ready at the rear with his guns turned toward the sky above the river.

There the gibbous moon suspended. A ragged coverlet of clouds. The stars veiled.

The father is uneasy in his single-sized bed, having been positioned just so by the daughter for the protection of certain of his parts. The mattress under him is one in motion, inflating and lifting him slightly with the undulations of perilous weather: leg-pelvis-chest-head, leg-pelvis-chest-head. He calls out from time to time. Turbulence! he says. Hang on, boys!

Wind comes in from the north, from far up-river, where the river is still a mountain rill, a feldspar brook. The big window rattles. Sudden cold. Snow clouds sail through the father's dreams.

A squadron of geese pass in formation, wings held wide from their bodies in the thrust thrust thrust of even beats. The bird in the lead tires and lags. He falls away. The slipstream takes him. Another gains and takes his place. Their soft black faces. Necks extended. Eyes of obsidian. Their forlorn hooting. Their hollow bones.

Waist gunner! See 'em? the father says. Nine o'clock high.

The daughter sleeps in her single-sized bed. Her bedroom has no view of the river. Her window looks out on homes enclosed in vinyl siding in suburban shades—putty tan, powder blue, charcoal, butter. Roofs are streaked with moss or darker rot. Lawns are decorated with the flora and fauna of fairytales. Geese gather at a doorstep, a gaggle in plastic. Crow-sized butterflies are staked into flowerbeds. Giant mushrooms sprout year round. A paint-chipped buck waits with lifted hoof, antlers atilt. A plaster doe is poised behind a bush. Rear windows overlook backyard ponds, hand-dug. Small waterfalls move with a motorized flow. Miniature windmills turn. A gnome fishes. Lot and block, plot and parcel—these commonplace properties harboring the creatures indigenous to dreams. Hers is the one devoid of ornament, the one with the grass in patches, the unruly hedge. Yard after yard, house after house, tight along the street.

The daughter sleeps alone in her single-sized bed, except when the man by the name of Joe and his lame-footed dog by the name of Johnny come to call as they have tonight, the man having tapped on her unhinged backdoor: Love, he said, how about dinner?—having hauled the lame-footed dog up the five stoop steps, having inquired as to the health of the father—her father—and having then consumed a makeshift meal in the daughter's kitchen—a stew of sorts: vegetables gone limp in the refrigerator crisper and a can of unexpired beans discovered in her dusty cupboard.

The man having fed the lame-footed dog a portion of the same.

With a spoon.

The man having attempted a patting of the daughter's clawing cats, thereby sustaining an assortment of superficial injuries and minor lacerations.

The man having whispered phrases of affection into a hairy ear and planting a goodnight kiss on the snout of the lame-footed dog who now sleeps at the foot of the single-sized bed, having tried out the fleece-lined dog bed on the floor and finding it unsatisfactory. The man beds down, having said Goodnight Love to the woman beside him, having checked the nose of the lame-footed dog for appropriate coldness, and having carefully arranged the daughter's shabby sheets and coverlet for proper covering and comfort of legs and back and shoulder and tail not withstanding.

Love, says Joe. Warm enough?

The father turns in his bed and talks in his sleep. He reaches around and pats the mattress, grabbing at the empty space beside him where the big woman used to be. Babs, the father says, his hand on the metal pan for pooping in. Babs, he says, is that you?

The big woman eats and talks in her sleep. Turkey club, she says. Heavy on the mayo.

A boat passes on the river and divides the reflected moon in its wake: moon on moon, on undulating moon.

The father slides his hand along the sheets. The clappered bell is missing or misplaced. Babs, he calls to the big woman spread upon the paisley in his old bedroom bed. Anyone? he says. Bombardier or Babs or gunner, the father says. Do you read? Bombardier, call in.

The big woman snores and talks in her sleep. Her bed is a barge, its consignment weighty. It carries her through the long cool night. The bedframe groans. The screw threads twist.

Babs, calls the father. I can't hear you. You're breaking up.

The father tugs on the sheets and tussles with the pillow. He unanchors a blanket so that he is on the loose in his bed. He slides against the rail. The pan for pooping clangs.

George shush! the big woman calls to the man in the rented bed.

Approaching target, the father says. Bombardier, call in.

The daughter shares her bed with the lame-footed dog and the cold-footed man. She tosses and talks in her sleep. Daddy, she says.

Shush now, says Joe to his lame-footed dog who sleeps while softly woofing and pawing in rhythm at the shabby sheets as it runs now sound of limb through a meadow of bright golden clover in pursuit of a slow-going lame-footed rabbit while the lame-footed dog snuffs and drools and muffly grunts with its mouth nearly shut, having a disorder of the musculature of mastication requiring it to be fed by hand, or more precisely, by hand-held spoon, having such deformity of jaw preventing a full and outright bark or a normal-dog yip or a lame-footed rabbit-hunting howl.

Johnnyboy? says Joe to his lame-footed dog. Shush, he says with a caress most kindly.

Joe? says the daughter to the man with the lame-footed dog, beside her in her bed.

George? says the big woman to the man in the railed-up rented bed a room away.

Daughter? says the father to the daughter not there.

The lame-footed dog sniffs and farts in his sleep.

Johnny, says the man to the lame-footed dog. No more beans.

The big woman talks and farts in her sleep.

Bombs away, the father says.

The lame-footed dog remorsefully whines and crawls his way northward under the comforter, up to a pillow. The daughter is nipped, nudged by a cold nose, pushed to the edge. She gets herself up and goes to the window. She looks out on the denizens of the neighborhood lawns: an artificial duck trailed by artificial ducklings; a plastic squirrel straddling a tree trunk. The painted buck stands in the shrubbery. The plaster doe waits. Her faux fawn sleeps. There the empty street in streetlight and shadow. A cat crosses. Something struggles in its mouth.

The dog bed is soft. And there is room enough if she bends her knees a bit. She notices that much hair has been shed. She brushes it away from the folds of fleece, and finds a rawhide chew, intact.

The father finds his clappered bell lodged between the mattress and the rail.

The big woman dreams a dinner bell is ringing. She rolls onto the platter of cheddar.

The moon descends—the last light on the water, on the face of the father, on the guns in the turrets, on the backs of the birds that follow the way the river goes. The father heads for home, full throttle.

The daughter dreams it is night in a forest. Moonlight slants through the canopy of trees. The floor is moss. There are ferns and pines. Fireflies. Mushrooms glow along the path. Roosting birds do not fly at her approach. Ducks on a pond pay her no notice, but go on sleeping with heads wing-tucked. Deer standing in the shafts of moonlight do not start and run. Until one sees her, stamps a hoof and snorts a warning. They all turn and lift their heads, ready for flight.

The daughter dreams she is calling after them, crying out. But they are bounding away from her, moving through the night, their bright tails rising and falling as they leap between the trees. Wait, she calls, but no sound comes. Wait—she wants to say—Not yet.

# TWO THINGS

I call my sister on the phone. No hello. What? she says.

Listen, I tell her. I'm working late. There's a couple of things that Daddy needs. Can you stop and pick them up? Just this once? Just two things.

What? she says.

First thing, I tell her: Seafoam Strips. Not the powder. The powder won't hold. And not the paste—it squishes all over. And not Tooth-Tight. Forget Tooth-Tight. Sure sure, if all he's eating is tapioca. But anything else—a bagel, for instance?—won't hold, so forget it. And no Zippy-Grip. Same kind of crap.

Mint-O-Dent?—she says—How about that?

Mint-O-Dent? I say. Not now, not ever. Just stick with the Seafoam. Seafoam Strips. Cut and stick. Simple as that. Seafoam Strips.

Second thing—I tell her: Probiotics. Get one that's Astromycetes. Not Acidophyllus. Not Lactobacilli. Get the capsules. Not the tablets. Not the generic. Get Astromycetes.

What about yogurt? is what she says. How about yogurt?

Yogurt? I tell her. Yogurt is crap. Hardly any Astromycetes in yogurt. Just get the kind called Astromycetes. Astromycetes. Not yogurt. No yogurt.

And that's it, I tell her. Just two things: Seafoam Strips. Astromycetes. Leave it on the kitchen table.

I get there late. Hi Daddy, I say. I see he's propped up in his rented bed.

Oh Pamela, he says. I head for the kitchen. The bag is on the kitchen table. I get the bag. I tear it open: vanilla yogurt and Mint-O-Dent.

I make some noise. I slam things around: a spatula, a pot. Whatever's in reach.

My father calls to me from the room where he lies in his bed. What was that? my father calls. Did I hear something break?

Pamela? he says. Is everything alright?

# MITZVAH

Down at the desk, they can always see you coming. They can see the visitors and the patients and the Call-Lights that blink above every door. There is little you can hide from the Desk People at the end of the corridor. There is little that they will not see.

Sometimes you must head down to the desk. You must speak with the Desk People about certain things, important things, such as What Is Going On With Your Father, and so forth. But they are very busy down at the desk. They are Short-Staffed—as you have been informed—so you must catch them during a Lull. If you head down to the desk at a Bad Time, a Desk Person will say: Sorry but this is a Bad Time.

Shift change is a Bad Time. Doctors at the desk is a Bad Time. Sylvia the Unit Clerk currently away from her desk is a Bad Time. So you must be patient and you must wait.

There are different things you can do while you wait for a Lull at the desk. You can watch the Medication Nurse push the Medication Cart. You can watch the Aide/Tech/Attendant push the Utility Cart. You can watch the old man in rumpled hospital pajamas walk his walker to the Snack & Soda Vending Station where he checks the slot for change.

You can stand nonchalantly in the doorway of Your Father's Room—Room 27—as if you are on the lookout for Housekeeping to show up and fill the toilet paper dispenser or as if you are hoping Dietary is about to deliver Your Father's meal-tray or the Volunteer with the smiley face button will soon be handing out complimentary newspapers to people too sick to sit in an upright position and read without passing out.

You wait for things to die down, down at the desk, or for Sylvia the Unit Clerk—who is currently away from her desk—to return. You wait for someone's Family Member—perhaps someone's son or daughter—a daughter like yourself perhaps—or then again a daughter not like yourself—to have come and gone with Concerns and Issues addressed. That is when a Desk Person is more likely to say May I Help You when you need to find out What Is Going On With Your Father and find out things, such things as: Is today the day Your Father is going for his scan thing? Such things as: Is his Doctor coming in or will it be the Covering Doctor who never met Your Father and will stand in the doorway of Room 27 for fifteen seconds and say: George Hirschberger? Are you Mr. Hirschberger? How Are You Doing Mr. Hirschberger? And such things as: Why does Your Father get OJ—which is high in potassium— on his meal tray when Your Father is Potassium Restricted, and why does he get granola crunch instead of oatmeal when his diet is Mechanical Soft, and why does the little menu-paper on his meal tray sometimes say Hirshbine, Gabriel and other times Hirshbine, Pincus—instead of Hirschberger, George. Those sorts of things.

You must be careful how you walk down to the desk. Marching down there in the middle of the corridor as if you had some Unreasonable Demand creates an Adversarial Relationship with the Desk People. Walking close to the wall, however, appears to be less threatening. Not sidling along with your back to the wall as if you were an Unstable Person. No, that would seem too crazy—but just off to the side. Nonchalant.

Though you have observed that the old man—the one with the walker—goes wherever he wants and it doesn't seem to matter. No one seems to pay him any mind. When he stops with his walker mid-corridor, bends over to pick up some bit of *schmutz* off the floor, and displays his suspiciously soiled pajama bottoms—no one tells him to get out of the way. When he sits in the Visitor Lounge at all hours, no one escorts him back to his room. No one puts him back to bed. No one seems to notice.

You, however, they notice. You they see coming down the corridor—they always do—but there are times you absolutely must go down to the desk. It is a bad idea to discuss your Concerns and Issues in Your Father's Room—27 W—W being Window, D being Door—especially in front of Your Father—for several reasons. The first reason being that Your Father thinks you are Making Too Much Of Everything. The second reason being that Your Father thinks that you are creating an Adversarial Relationship with the Desk People, and he doesn't want to be labeled a Complainer. The third reason being that you know that when a static sort of noise comes out of the little speaker on the wall, the Desk People are listening in on your conversations with Your Father. So you do not discuss Issues or Concerns with Your Father or even in Your Father's Room.

In general, you discuss more Innocuous Topics with Your Father. Such as: Will the Rangers make the playoffs? Such as: How hard it is to find a parking spot, or what the weather is like outside? You try not to discuss What Is Going On With Your Father with Your Father, because lately What Is Going On does not seem to be very good. You do not discuss how his bones ache from being in bed. You do not mention the red spot on his butt. You do not discus his breathing problem or his heart thing or his blood trouble. You do not discuss anything Life Or Death. If Life Or Death Topics come up, you start talking about things outside the window, even though there's not much of a view. Look, you say—See those trees across the parking lot? They're already changing color, don't you think? Or: Look at that cloud, you say—cumulonimbus, isn't it? We're supposed to be getting some rain.

Today there are certain things you must discuss down at the desk. You peek out of the doorway of Room 27. You wait until you see that other Family Members have dispersed with their Concerns and Issues addressed, that the patients' buzzers are not buzzing, that the patients' Call-Lights are not blinking, and that the Nurses have finished speaking to the Doctors about Medical Matters such as the benefits of consuming eight glasses of water a day not counting caffeinated, or the lack of decent Thai restaurants within walking distance. You wait until the Nurses are having fun spinning around in their swivel chairs, comparing shades of nail polish, and you make your move.

You head down to the desk. You pass the Visitor Lounge. You pass the Snack & Soda Vending Station. The old man is there, leaning on his walker and pressing the coin-return button. You see that his hospital pajamas are very rumpled. His hair is not combed. His beard is straggly. He pokes his finger into the coin return slot. Don't bother, he tells you. I already checked.

You keep on. Past the Staff Only Pantry and the Staff Only Bathroom. Past the elevator. You arrive at the desk.

A Nurse in a swivel chair makes eye contact. This is very good. Maybe she is new. You see that her nametag says Patrice Something RN, though you are not sure of the Something because you cannot Gaze at her nametag. Nametag Gazing is frowned upon. Verboten. This is because nametag wearers suspect you are attempting to remember an actual name for if-and-when you make an Official Complaint or try to pin something on them. Although you never would, because Official Complaints backfire, create Adversarial Relationships, result in Retaliation and more Unpleasantness for Your Father, and so forth. So while nametag Gazing is discouraged, nametag Glancing is perfectly permissible.

May I Help You? says Patrice.

Well yes, you say, I hope you can help me. And you tell Patrice that Your Father has not been getting the correct meal tray. Your Father, you tell her, has been getting a meal tray destined for someone by the name of Hirshbine, Gabriel or Hirshbine, Pincus and not Hirschberger, George—not Your Father in 27 W.

It's a spelling error, says Patrice. Hirshbine, Hirschberger—all the same. It's what Dietary calls a Typo, says Patrice.

Now you are in a bad spot because you will have to Reiterate Your Concerns and possibly challenge The Typo Explanation.

Well—you tell Patrice in your least challenging voice—you are concerned because Your Father is losing weight. He's not getting the right food, you tell Patrice. He's not getting the kind of food he's supposed to be getting.

He's getting the right food, says Patrice.

You are now in an even worse spot—Reiteration failing—and it is time for a new tactic: Expressing Concern For Others. Maybe—you tell Patrice—maybe the other patient—this Mr. Hirshbine—isn't getting his food either. Could you check?

Check what? says Patrice

Check on the Typo, you say.

Patrice then lets loose with a big Adversarial Relationship Sigh and picks up a clipboard. She flips the through the pages. Hirshbine, Hirshbine, says Patrice while she flips. Nope, she says. No Hirsh-*bine* on record. We do, however, have a Hirsch-*berger*.

Right, you say. That's My Father, you tell Patrice.

Hirshbine or Hirschberger? says Patrice. Who's Your Father? Which?

You head back along the corridor. You pass the elevator and the Staff Only Bathroom and the Staff Only Pantry. You pass the Medication Nurse pushing the Medication Cart, and the Aide/Tech/Attendant pushing the Utility Cart. Next is the Snack & Soda Vending Station. You see that the old man is there with his walker and he is eating a Vending Station snack.

Expired, he says holding up a little bag of barbeque chips. Not kosher, he says, and loaded with sodium but keep it to yourself. And he gives you a little wink.

I will, you say.

You suspect that the entire snack selection is expired. Not that there's much of a soda selection either. In fact, the soda selection is limited to one kind of soda: Pepsi-Cola. Only Pepsi-Cola. And Pepsi-Cola you happen to hate.

Black cherry, Cel-Ray, or orange? the old man says, nodding to the Vending Station. On me, he says.

And since it's all Pepsi-Cola and nothing but, you go along. Sure, you say, OK. Black cherry would be nice.

Because a black cherry *would* be nice and you have no idea what Cel-Ray is anyway.

One black cherry coming up, the old man says, and with that, he keeps on holding the walker with one hand and smacks the front of the Snack & Soda Vending Station with the other. And not even a very hard smack.

The Snack & Soda Vending Station makes a rumbling sort of noise and the soda light flashes. You hear a thud-thud-thud—and a can of black cherry pops into the chute.

There you go, the old man says, handing it over. Nice and cold.

He wipes his hand off on his pajama top. Hirshbine, Gabriel, 57 W, the old man says and puts his hand out for you to shake.

Hirshbine?

But most of my associates call me Gabe, he says. Or Pincus, if you prefer.

You look at the hand of Hirshbine, Gabriel or Hirshbine, Pincus—the hand he has extended for you to shake. It is a very wrinkly old hand. Wrinkly and spotty. And not a very clean-looking hand. There seems to be some kind of dirt under his nails—you hate to think what. This hand of Hirshbine is not a hand you would like to shake. But you do.

Mr. Hirshbine—you say—My Father is George Hirschberger and he's getting your meal tray; he's getting your food by mistake.

Ah! says Hirshbine. So it shouldn't go to waste. And please, he says, better you should call me Gabe. Or Pincus. Either.

You head on into Your Father's Room.

Your Father is sitting up in his bed, eating a blintz. Blueberry. Sour cream on the side.

Where'd you get that? you ask Your Father.

The Doctor—you just missed him, Your Father says.

The Doctor? you say. Doctors don't just show up handing out blintzes.

Then some guy, he says.

Which guy? you say.

Some old guy, Your Father says.

Transport arrives with a wheelchair. The Transport guy looks at the card in his hand. He looks at you. You George? he says.

No I'm not George, you say. Do I look like a George? I'm George's daughter. George Hirschberger is My Father, you tell the Transport guy.

Your Father tries to sit up a bit in his bed, and gives the Transport guy a feeble little wave hello. I'm George, he says.

A crackling noise and the sound of static come out from the intercom grill, and then the voice of a Desk Person: Transport? That you in 27?

Yeah, says the Transport Guy. I'm here for Hirschberger, George.

No, says the Desk Person, not Hirschberger.

My card says pick up Hirschberger, says the Transport guy.

No, says the Desk Person. Disregard. It's a Typo.

There are New Issues, as well as some of the Old Issues, you must address down at the desk. And sure, sure—Unpleasantness will ensue. But you have to take your chances. You head on down to the desk.

You pass the Visitor Lounge and the Snack & Soda Vending Station. You pass the Medication Cart and the Utility Cart, the Staff Only Pantry, the Staff Only Bathroom, and the elevator. You arrive at the desk.

You think that this is not a Bad Time, since Sylvia the Unit Clerk is at the desk. But Sylvia is not answering her phone. Sylvia is allowing her answering machine to pick up and say: I Am Currently Away From My Desk.

There are Nurses at the desk. However, the Nurses are occupied with Hospital Topics, such as which Doctor has the most charisma, and which one has the least, and which nurse would *do* the doctor with the least for, say, a million dollars? And you do not say Excuse Me, because Excuse Me can be considered an Interruption or an Offensive Remark. And you do not say Can Someone Help Me?—as that would imply

Impatience when you already know the desk is Short-Staffed. And anyway, you understand that Good-Natured Banter among the Nurses helps relieve the Pressures and Stresses of their jobs.

Doctors arrive at the desk. But it would not help to ask a Doctor about What's Going On With Your Father. The Doctors are discussing their own Medical Topics: the failure rate of penile implants; the elimination of algae in their waiting room fish tanks; how tasteless store-bought tomatoes are right now even though they look so red and shiny. So you nicely stand and wait. You are not sighing loudly or clearing your throat. You are not clicking clicking clicking a ballpoint pen, not putting your finger on the hang-up button while Desk People are talking on the phone. You are not Making A Scene. Not saying Can't I Get Some Fucking Help Here? Not shoving a computer monitor with attached mouse and keyboard off the desk and into someone's lap. No. You wait.

The Doctors disperse. A Nurse sits down in the swivel chair farthest away from you. Her nametag says Enid Something RN. Enid does not look up.

Hi Enid! you say. As if you and Enid Something are old pals.

Enid looks up.

Can I help you? she says.

Well yes! you say. I hope you can help me. My Father was supposed to have a blood test before breakfast, but no one came to take his blood. Is it possible that someone might have possibly, inadvertently, unintentionally, accidentally forgotten to take his blood? Because now My Father's lunch tray has arrived—well, not exactly *his* lunch tray. *A* lunch tray. Someone else's lunch tray. And My Father is still afraid to eat and mess up the blood test.

Eat, not eat—it doesn't matter, says Enid.

Now you are in a bad spot again because you happen to know that this blood-test eating-thing *does* matter, and you will have to Reiterate and Challenge. However, Feigning Stupidity at this point can also be effective, so you must present yourself as a confused, ignorant, Overly Concerned Family Member relying entirely on her professional expertise.

You say: Don't some tests get messed up if the person eats? I don't really understand all this Technical Stuff like you Nurses do. I'm just going by what the Doctor told My Father.

You throw in that thing about the Doctor because this can be Intimidating and yet Productive.

Who's Your Father? Enid says.

You head back. You pass the elevator. You pass the Staff Only Bathroom and the Staff Only Pantry. You pass the parked Utility Cart with no Aide/Tech/Attendant in attendance. You pass the Medication Cart and the Medication Nurse. Next is the Snack & Soda Vending Station. Next is the Visitor Lounge.

Mr. Hirshbine is in there, leaning back comfortably in a vinyl chair. He is drinking a Cel-Ray Soda. He has an unlit cigar in his mouth.

Good evening Mr. Hirshbine, you say.

Well Hello—says Hirshbine—You're the daughter, correct?

Yes, you say. I'm the daughter.

A very good evening to you, says Hirshbine. And give my regards to Your Father.

Yes thank you, you tell Hirshbine.

One thing before you go, says Hirshbine. I was wondering, he says, holding the cigar in his fingers. Would you happen to have a light?

You head on into Your Father's Room.

Your Father is sitting up in his bed with a dish of gefilte fish on his bedside table. Horseradish on the side.

Where'd you get that? you ask Your Father.

Some old guy, he says.

Some old guy? you say. Some old guy giving out gefilte fish?

Right, Your Father says.

So this old guy—what did he say? you ask him.

He said it was a *mitzvah*, Your Father tells you, and digs in.

Transport arrives with a wheelchair. It's the same Transport guy, but the wheelchair is strapped-up with a green oxygen tank and plastic tubing and a clear plastic mask.

The Transport guy looks at the card in his hand and he looks at Your Father and says: You Hirshbine? Time for your scan thing, Mr. Hirshbine!

Hold on, you tell the Transport guy. This is not Mr. Hirshbine. This is Mr. Hirschberger. George Hirschberger.

No I don't think so, says the Transport guy. He's Hirshbine, Gabriel. I've got it right here: Hirshbine, Gabriel. Let's go Gabe! the Transport guy says. Hop aboard!

But I'm George, Your Father tells the Transport guy.

This is George—My Father—you tell the Transport guy. And this room is 27 W.

The Transport guy backs up the wheelchair a little and sticks his head outside the door. He checks the room number on the wall. He takes some white cards from his pocket and shuffles them around. So where is Hirshbine, Gabriel? he says and he looks at another card. Or Hirshbine, Pincus, he says— Where's he?

And right then comes the static noise, the crackling from the little intercom grill and the voice of a Desk Person: Transport, that you in 27?

Yeah, says the Transport guy into the intercom. Where's this Hirshbine fella at?

Hold on, says the Desk Person. We're checking.

So you hold on. You and the Transport guy hold on while they're checking. The Transport guy looks out the window. Nice day, isn't it? he says.

Sure is, you say.

Look at them clouds, says the Transport guy. Ever see clouds like that?

You look.

That one there, says the Transport guy. That one there looks like something. Like cotton candy maybe or a blob of sour cream, he says.

There's more static noise. The voice of the Desk Person comes back on the intercom. Who's it you're looking for? Hirshbine? Is that the name?

The Tranport guy checks his card. Yeah, that's it. Hirshbine, he says.

There's no Hirshbine, says the desk Person. Probably a Mix-Up. Or could be a Discharge or maybe an Expired.

Fine by me, the Transport guy says into the intercom.

Have a nice day, he tells you and rolls the wheelchair out the door.

They always see you heading down the corridor, heading for the desk. And it is becoming more difficult to find out What Is Going On With Your Father because it seems that what is going on with him is not very good. And it is becoming more difficult to find a Nurse at the desk who will help you find out What Is Going On because—as you have been informed—it is now Sylvia the Unit Clerk who is supposed to provide Visitor Assistance if she is not currently away from her desk. Sylvia is supposed to say May I Help You while the Nurses are busy with Nursing Functions such as: the prevention of red spots on patients' butts, or administration of medications from the Medication Cart, or ordering take-out Chinese.

And sometimes, these Nursing Functions can be quite complicated. Ordering take-out Chinese for example. This can be tricky because free delivery is only for orders over $15, and it takes a while for enough people to agree that they are in the mood for Szechuan Spicy Wonton or Kung Pao Delight.

So you decide to find out about Your Father from the Aides/Techs/Attendants because they are more Hands On. And you know which ones are Aides/Techs/Attendants because they wear their nametags turned around so you can't see their names, making Nametag Gazing not an Issue. But often it is difficult to locate the Aides/Techs/Attendants. They don't hang around the desk. In fact, where they actually are seems to be unclear. Sometimes they can be found going slowly up and down the corridor, pushing Utility Carts stacked with linen and waterproof pads and butt-wiping cloths and butt-cleaning sprays and butt-soothing lotions to prevent red spots. Other times they are hiding out in a patient's room with the door closed so it appears as if they are Providing Privacy—giving a patient a bed-bath or a bed-pan or so forth—when what they are actually doing is watching *Dancing With The Stars* on the patient's wall-mount TV—when a patient would rather be watching something else—such as Hockey Playoffs, for example. And since you can't find a single Aide/Tech/Attendant anywhere, this may be one of those times.

You have no choice—You must head down to the desk. You pass the Visitor Lounge and the Snack & Soda Vending Station. You pass the Utility Cart.

You see Mr. Hirshbine is midway down the corridor, leaning on his walker beside the Medication Nurse and her Medication Cart. You see that he is opening and closing the little drawers of medications. And this you find absolutely amazing, because—as you have been previously informed—interfering with a Nursing Function such as administration of medications from the Nursing Cart—or even getting *near* the Medication Cart—is absolutely Verboten.

But there is Hirshbine, mumbling to himself, rummaging around in the Medication Cart drawers. And this is even more amazing: the Medication Nurse doesn't seem to care, not a whit. Not even when he sticks in his fingers—those fingers of his—and pokes around.

He picks out some pills. He slams the drawer shut.

What's wrong Mr. Hirshbine? you say, not getting too close.

A headache you wouldn't believe, says Hirshbine.

~

You proceed down the corridor, expecting some degree of Unpleasantness down at the desk. You suspect that you have been labeled a Complainer. Which could be why it is so hard to find out What Is Going On With Your Father or have your Concerns and Issues addressed. Which would be completely unfair. Because, after all, you have made every effort to show your appreciation. You have, in fact, purchased snacks for the Staff. That nice cookie assortment, for example. And the giant jar of salsa and big bags of multigrain organic chips. And you always write a note: Many Thanks From George Hirschberger - Room 27 W. You write this for Your Father because his hand shakes when he is writing. You write this so when they see Your Father's Call-Light on they will remember the snacks and will say That's Who Gave Us The Snacks and they will hurry in to see What's Going On With Your Father. And they will treat him—treat Your Father—with kindness. Sure.

In addition to the snacks, you have consistently said Thank You for every kindness—few and far between as they may be—and have never ever worded a request as a Demand or even as a Threatening Direct Question. You have never said, for example: Who the hell left My Father lying in piss? Don't you know he can get a red spot lying in piss? No. You say: My Father seems to have spilled his urinal—as if it is all Your Father's fault. You say: Is there someone available that can *help me* clean him up?—as if you are perfectly happy to help them do *their* jobs. As if you were not a family member, not a daughter. As if you are absolutely willing to wait and to give them a hand because—as you have been informed—Your Father Is Not The Only Patient On This Floor.

You have been willing to roll up your sleeves and pitch right in and help these hefty women, these big-bicepted rubber-gloved beefy bitches who are half your age and double your size. You have shown them that you still have some strength left in your post middle-aged bones when you reposition Your Father since he seems to be getting weaker and he seems to be having more trouble moving himself around. That you are more than happy to be washing Your Father's dick and the crack where the poop and pee collect since he is having more trouble with poop and pee. That you have no qualms, none at all, and no shame whatsoever about any of it, and neither does he, neither does Your Father. And sometimes when his butt is hurting or his bones are aching and Your Father needs rolling over toward the window, you talk about the things he can see out there—outside the window—not that there is much to see. You say: Look at that big tree out there? Oak, I think. Or: Did you ever see such a skinny new moon? Or: Doesn't that cloud look like a person? And you hope that he is thinking about trees and moons and clouds, and not about his daughter doing these things. And that he is not ashamed—that Your Father is not embarrassed or ashamed at all, no not one bit.

You continue on down to the desk. You fear something Unpleasant could happen. Or Adversarial. There have been times when you get close to the desk and you can hear Desk People speaking quietly—as if they don't want you to hear—don't want you to know What Is Going On With Your Father.

As luck would have it, a Lucky Thing happens on your way to the desk: the Evening Overhead Announcement comes on. Attention All Visitors, Visiting Hours Are Now Over! Drive

Safely And Have A Nice Evening! So you pretend to make a beeline for the elevator in a slightly hurrying yet nonchalant manner on the right side of the corridor—the elevator side. Going Down? you say to the people in the elevator, and Hold That Please? and you quick feint to the left, pull an about-face to the desk, and bingo: you're standing right in front of a Desk Person—a Nurse sitting in a swivel chair.

Her nametag says Meredith Something RN, and since you have abruptly landed here right in front of her, Meredith Something has no choice but to look up and say: May I Help You?

How are you this evening?—you say.

Meredith does not say how she is this evening. No. Instead she says How May I Help You—adding *How* this time in a broken-record sort of voice which you take to mean: don't assume this pleasant how-are-you shit will work on me so get to the fucking point because you heard the fucking announcement: Visiting Hours Are Now Over.

Well, you tell Meredith, the first thing is you would like Your Father to get his own meal-tray, a meal-tray with his name on it, not the name Hirshbine, Gabriel or Hirshbine, Pincus.

Someone already checked into that, says Meredith. They told me that somebody already told you: It's a Typo, she says. Anything else?

Well yes, one other thing, and you tell Meredith that you try to get here at mealtimes to help Your Father with his meal tray—well not actually *his* meal tray but *a* meal tray—but sometimes you can't get here on time. Your Father has trouble with his hands, you tell her. Your Father's hands shake. And tonight Your Father couldn't open his milk container, couldn't unwrap his disposable napkin, couldn't lift the cover off his Heat-Keeper Dinner Dish, couldn't get the top off the tapioca cup, couldn't pop the lid off his Heat-Keeper Coffee Container, couldn't peel the little square of paper from the pat of Butter Substitute, couldn't hold his crappy plastic disposable fork in his hand since he never received the Adaptive-Device Fork he was supposed to get in order to dig into the slab of non-kosher meatloaf, reconstituted instant potatoes, and the gray-tinted green beans. And since you, his daughter, arrived too late to flip/uncover/unlid/peel or pop—since you didn't get here in time to unwrap/chop/feed or cut, Dietary came and carted away his meal tray totally untouched. Your Father didn't get any dinner! Hard to believe, isn't it, that such a thing as this—a patient not getting nourishment—could occur in a Cutting Edge, JD Powers Award-Winning Top Hospital such as this. So you made an attempt to find Your Father's Nurse yourself. You really did. You checked the wipe-off whiteboard in Your Father's Room where the Nurse writes her name with big red markers so the patient knows who his Nurse is, even though the wipe-off whiteboard is clear across the room and too far away for Your Father to see. And when you checked the wipe-off whiteboard, it said YOUR NURSE TODAY IS: JUDY.

So you looked for JUDY. You really did, but you couldn't find any JUDY anywhere. No sign of a JUDY. This JUDY is nowhere to be found, you say.

And Meredith Something RN at the desk looks at you and says:

Maybe JUDY is On Break.

Maybe JUDY is the Float and not the Regular JUDY.

The whiteboard JUDY could actually be JUDITH.

JUDY was yesterday and the whiteboard wasn't updated and the big red marker is out of ink.

So, you say, Who Is It Today? because you really need to find out who can help Your Father at mealtimes when you are late.

And before this Meredith Something RN can say Who's Your Father—which is what they always say—though you are sure they actually do know who Your Father is but they say it anyway just to Bust Your Balls if you had balls—before she has time to pull the Who's Your Father crap, you beat Meredith Something RN to the punch. You pipe right up and say: My Father is George Hirschberger in Room 27 W.

And then, as if you have some degree of Short Term Memory Loss and have forgotten that you have been down to the desk loads of times asking What Is Going On With Your Father, or as if you are accusing a Nurse of not remembering that for the past nine days Your Father has been in Room 27—27 W in fact—W for Window and not D for door—as if it were all of this—this Meredith looks up and says: I *Know* Who Your Father Is.

You head back to Your Father's Room. You pass the elevator. Then the Staff Only Bathroom. Then the Staff Only Pantry. You pass the Medication Nurse pushing the Medication Cart. You pass an Aide/Tech/Attendant doing nothing. Then there's the Snack & Soda Vending Station. Then there's the Visitor Lounge.

Mr. Hirshbine is in there, lounging on one of the vinyl chairs. He is looking very comfortable in those same old pajamas. He has his feet up on another chair. He is drinking an orange soda. He has his unlit cigar in his mouth.

And now there is something else Mr. Hirshbine is doing. Mr. Hirshbine is taking a pack of matches out of his pajama-top pocket, and then Mr. Hirshbine is lighting his unlit cigar.

No one comes running down from the desk. No one is shouting: Put That Out. No one is making an overhead No Smoking Announcement.

And Mr. Hirshbine is smoking his cigar.

You return to Your Father's Room. Your Father is sitting up in bed and he is eating lox on a sesame-seed bagel. Cream cheese. Slice of onion.

Don't ask, Your Father says.

Transport arrives. It is the same Transport guy. He sees you and he says: You again.

Looking for Gabriel Hirshbine? you say.

No, says the Tranport guy. Definitely not.

How about Pincus? Pincus Hirshbine. You looking for him?

Hell no, says the Transport guy. Don't even mention Pincus Hirshbine, he says. Don't get me started about him.

Now you absolutely must get to the desk because there is a new Concern that must be addressed. This new Concern concerns Facilities Management and/or Maintenance and you happen to know they are Unavailable On Weekends. And here it is already Friday late afternoon.

You are concerned because Your Father's Call-Light is not working. No light flashes outside Room 27 when you push the bedside button. When Your Father pushed and pushed and pushed the bedside button because you were not here, because you were late, because he couldn't reach the urinal—oops oops oops he had an Accident in the bed. And you are concerned because lying in urine can cause a red spot.

So you head for the desk.

You pass the Visitor Lounge and the Snack & Soda Vending Station. You pass the Medication Cart with no Medication Nurse and the Utility Cart with no Aide/Tech/Attendant. You notice that there isn't much Staff around—probably a combination of the weekend plus Short-Staffed.

You pass the Staff Only Pantry, the Staff Only Bathroom, the elevator. You arrive at the desk.

The Nurse is not looking up. She is doing Pretend Paperwork. You wait. Gazing is Verboten, but she is not looking up. So you are able to Gaze at her nametag for a few seconds longer than is usually permitted and you see it says: Judy Gomznftic RN. You wonder if this is possibly the wipe-off whiteboard JUDY, but that was yesterday. You consider addressing this Judy, but you are likely to mispronounce her nearly vowel-less last name and possibly create an Adversarial Relationship with Judy—which should be avoided just in case she winds up on Your Father's wipe-off whiteboard and decides upon Retaliation. So you just say: Judy?

But Judy does not look up. She does not say, Yes! Hello! I'm Judy, or even May I Help You?

No, this Judy keeps right on writing and she says:

I am not the person taking care of Your Father.

Your Father has been assigned to some other Nurse.

You need to talk to someone else about Your Father, not me.

Oh! You say. Well this is not actually a Nursing Function Issue. It is more of Facilities Management or a Maintenance Issue. And you tell her that Your Father's Call-Light is not working, and it being Friday night and Facilities Management or Maintenance being Unavailable On Weekends, you would really like to have his Call-Light working. In case he needs something. In case he can't reach his urinal. In case he has an Accident in the bed or he spills his urinal and the bed gets wet which can make a red spot or make a red spot redder. In case he needs to roll over. In case his meal-tray does not come and no one happens by with a blintz or a bagel or a latke or a noodle kugel or some gefilte fish. In case Something Is Going On With Your Father. Something with his bones or his blood or his breathing, or something unforeseen.

And finally, this Judy—this other Judy, this not-me Judy—this Judy Gomznftic, Judy Gomznfuckit, Judy Gofuckyourself-whydontyou—she puts down her Pretend Paperwork and she looks up at you and she says: Who's Your Father?

You head back to Your Father's Room. You pass the elevator, the Staff Only Bathroom, the Staff Only Pantry. You pass the Medication Cart and the Medication Nurse. You pass an Aide/Tech/Attendant not pushing the Utility Cart.

Next is the Snack & Soda Vending Station. Next is the Visitor Lounge.

It is dim in there—in the Visitor Lounge. Mr. Hirshbine is in there standing at the window in the last light of the day.

You can see that Mr. Hirshbine is wearing fresh pajamas. His hair has been combed. His beard has been trimmed. His hands are clean.

And you see that Mr. Hishbine has a prayer shawl draped across his shoulders. You see that he has candles. You see that he has matches.

The sun is just near setting. The hills beyond the parking lot almost seem to glow.

It is colder now—you know it: by the gusts that are rattling the window and by the leaves that are rising from the trees.

Mr. Hirshbine sees you in the doorway. Ah—the daughter—says Hirshbine. He gives a nod towards the window. Such a view—he says—you shouldn't miss it.

You look out past the window, past the parking lot, to the hills and sky. You see that the clouds are low and moving. That they have turned the colors of the leaves that are turning early. That they are impaled on shafts of gold, and through and through are pierced with light.

Shabbat Shalom, says Hirshbine and he turns back to the window.

He picks up a candle. He strikes a match.

There are no stars—not yet—but a crescent of moon is rising. And it is bright, and as pale as bone.

# RECOGNIZABLE CONSTELLATIONS AND FAMILIAR OBJECTS OF THE NIGHT SKY IN EARLY SPRING

*To all, welcome.*

*Our program will be starting momentarily, so find your places.*

*The first stars of the evening are beginning to appear.*

*We have a number of small children in our audience tonight.*

*Please remember that they must remain quiet and seated at all times during the presentation.*

*Your eyes will adjust as the doors close behind you and the lights slowly dim.*

*There will be ample time to grow accustomed to the dark.*

Hello? the daughter says. Hello?

Is this the daughter? The adult daughter?

Yes, the daughter says. This is.

I am speaking to the daughter then?

Yes yes, the daughter says. I am the daughter.

Apologies for the lateness of the hour, but we are calling with some news.

What is it? the daughter says.

Were you already awake? You answered so quickly.

Please tell me, the daughter says. What is this about?

Your father.

Yes? the daughter says.

*With the vernal equinox upon us, it is time we gaze upon the skies of early spring. On clear nights, far from city glare and streetlights, we may view some of the most recognizable constellations and familiar objects of the night sky.*

*Follow the pointer, if you will, to our first constellation: Orion—the hunter. Here, the three bright stars in a row—the prominent Belt of Orion, with Betelgeuse in close proximity. And here, near the celestial equator, the hunting dogs of the constellations Canis Minor and Canis Major, although both are somewhat obscured by clouds of interstellar dust.*

Tell me, the daughter says.

Certainly. You are, after all, the daughter. And first on our list for notification.

Notification? the daughter says.

But before I begin, I must ask: Are you sitting down?

Please, the daughter says.

Sitting near a window, perhaps? Possibly awake at this hour and watching the sky? On a clear night such as this, one might.

Oh tell me, the daughter says.

*Let us now look to the north and the conspicuous constellation Ursa Major, the Great Bear—visible throughout the year in most of the Northern Hemisphere. Within it, there—the Big Dipper, a well-known formation glittering anew. During the nights of winter, it bordered the horizon, but now it nears the zenith of the sky.*

*Again, following the pointer, visualize Ursa Minor, commonly re-*
*ferred to as The Little Dipper. There, at the handle we find Polaris, the*
*pivot of the stars. It is well visible to the naked eye and for ancient naviga-*
*tors, seafarers, and fliers, it is a familiar old friend.*

Regarding your father, as I said. We have some news.

What is it? the daughter says.

Your father has been found.

He was missing? the daughter says.

Among the missing. In a way, yes he was.

I hadn't been informed, the daughter says. I hadn't been told.

We usually don't. In cases such as his, there are frequent false alarms.

He was missing before? the daughter says.

Not actually missing.

He's never been lost, the daughter says. He always finds his way.

Not actually lost. Just here or there. You know how he is. Off on a jaunt. A short flight.

A flight? the daughter says.

He flies, does he not? A war, way back. That sort of thing.

He did, the daughter says. He used to fly.

Well, that would explain it. Why we find him where we do.

Where have you found him? the daughter says.

You're going to laugh when I tell you where.

Where? the daughter says.

Various places. Strolling about. The grounds. The roof.

The roof? the daughter says. But I should have been called.

There was no need. He's frequently there, viewing the sky and sighting stars for celestial navigation. What matters most is that he has been found. Your father has been found.

Where? the daughter says. Where was he found?

As I mentioned, various places.

Tell me then, the daughter says.

We found your father climbing from his bed, tossing away his pillow, pulling off the bed sheets, escaping past the rail. We found your father with the cord and the button that we put in his hands for calling for help when he needs to drink or pass his water or eat or turn in his bed—pulled from the wall, all in a tangle.

He has trouble with the call-light, the daughter says. He twists up the cord. He can't push the button.

We've never heard him complain of any trouble. We never heard him ask for any help.

No, he wouldn't, the daughter says. He doesn't like to ask.

Without asking, how could we know?

You could go and check, the daughter says. See what he needed.

But you weren't here, isn't that correct? He waited for your visit, but you weren't here when we found your father slipping out of his bed with the cord in his hands sparking and coiling and dangerously hissing.

You weren't here when we found your father with the cord and the button winding in his hands, in motion in his hands, as he headed past the laundry room where we keep the sheets and pillowcases and the waterproof pads; passing by the cart stacked with disposable diapers and plastic bedpans; stealing past the pantry and the shelves stocked with tea bags and packets of sugar and creamer and instant coffee and the boxes of broth and cans of milkshake. You weren't here when we found your father leaving the premises with a snake in his hands, heading for the distant globular cluster just opposite Orion before he descends—a man with a serpent twisting in his fists.

Where? the daughter says. Where did you say?

We found your father in the constellation Serpus, clearly visible northwest of the center of the Milky Way.

Impossible, the daughter says.

Quite possible, in fact. Especially on nights that are moonless and clear, away from city glare. Between latitudes plus and minus eighty.

No, the daughter says. You must be mistaken. My father has a deadly fear of snakes.

Apparently not. Not one bit. We have found him to be fearless at times. We have found him in the most unlikely of places. And I know you're going to laugh when you hear.

Where? the daughter says. Tell me where.

We found your father rising from the chair where we sometimes make him sit. He was overturning his bedside table. He was reaching for the cup with the flexible straw. He was reaching for the water we keep just out of reach.

I'm sure I explained how his hands tremble, the daughter says.

You might have explained, but you weren't here. He needed a drink of water, and you weren't here.

I know I told everyone about the paper cups, the daughter said. How the paper cups are impossible to hold. How he needs a sippy-cup.

You might have told everyone, but you weren't here. You weren't around when we found your father spilling the water from his cup, sliding on the slick floor and stepping through the wet.

You weren't here when we found your father with his empty cup in the constellation Aquarius. He was filling his cup at the Water Bearer's jar. He was taking a drink with his flexible straw. He was rinsing out his mouth and putting in his teeth. Most recently, we believe, he had lost his teeth.

Aquarius? the daughter says.

A familiar constellation just South of Pegasus and bordering Pisces.

I hadn't known, the daughter says.

Aquarius? Oh yes. Easily recognizable throughout the Northern Hemisphere just along the plane of the ecliptic. Visible at latitudes between plus sixty-five degrees and minus ninety.

Are you quite sure? the daughter says.

Of the latitude location? There is no doubt.

That his teeth have been found, the daughter says.

Of course they were found. Most certainly found.

Where were they found? the daughter says.

You're going to laugh when I tell you where.

Tell me, the daughter says.

We found your father's teeth in the pocket of his pajamas, mixed up with pennies he liked to pick up, rattling around with pebbles he had found. We found his teeth, but a molar had been chipped. An incisor had been cracked.

We found your father's teeth inside a compass case, wrapped in a flight plan, tied with a boot lace, tucked inside a no-skid sock, tossed down the laundry chute. We found your father's teeth on his bedside table, on his tray of food, hidden under a covered dish, next to the low-salt potatoes, the low-sodium applesauce, the low-potassium meatloaf he left untouched to be tossed out with the leftovers.

We found your father climbing out the window, crossing the parking lot, heading past the area set aside for visitor parking and the spaces reserved for the medical director, the nurse in charge, the head of housekeeping, the cook, the dietitian, the supervisor for recreational activities, and the chief of rehabilitation and occupational therapy. Past the spaces set aside for fifteen-minute ambulance drop-off and the in-and-out mortuary pick-ups. We found your father past the no parking signs and the loading zone, past the paved path for rolling walkers and quad-cane users. We found your father out past the shed where we keep the rakes for raking and the shovels for digging, the electric clippers for trimming the hedge, and the hose for watering the grounds and hosing down wheelchairs. Past the fenced-in enclosure where we keep the trashcans and garbage; past the containers for galactic debris and the bins for recyclables; beyond the chain link gate that keeps out the animals. The rogue bears and the bold raccoons. The rats, mice, and meadow voles. The odd fox or occasional skunk. The feral cats. The scavenger dogs.

We found your father sitting in a dumpster. He had found the covered dish that contained his teeth. He was poking through the bags of rotted kitchen refuse. Searching for green peas left in the cast-off pea pods and sorting through the peelings of potatoes and carrots. Fly-specked cutlets. Wormy apples. Maggoty chicken parts and patties of chopped chuck. We found him picking through the whole meals that are slid or scraped from plates and platters—entire dinners left untouched on the over-bed tables of the paralyzed and the incapacitated unable to reach their meal trays. Unable to lift the hot-lids from dishes or open the plastic wrappings of their sanitized utensils. Unable to pry apart the cartons of sugar-free chocolate milk or two-percent skim. Unable to hold a fork or a cup or a sippy-cup or a spoon. Unable to swallow.

We found your father sitting in a dumpster with a small foraging dog that was tearing up the trash. They were sharing a discarded brisket and a crust of potpie. The dog was yapping. Your father was eating and telling the dog: Shh.

I don't think so, the daughter says.

Oh we are quite certain it was Canis Minor—the little dog that trails Orion to the east.

I doubt it, really, the daughter says. My father has a dislike of dogs. A fear of dogs. Small dogs, yappy dogs. Little dogs especially.

We were very sure it was Canis Minor—visible at latitudes between ninety and seventy-five degrees. Brightest during the month of March.

This is March, the daughter says.

And once we found his teeth exactly were he left them. They were right there in his mouth the whole time. He had just forgotten.

He needs his teeth, the daughter says. He needs them to eat.

We are aware.

And he needs to be fed, says the daughter.

Requiring meal-time assistance is the way we word it.

He misses his mouth when he holds the spoon, says the daughter. The food goes all over.

We've never heard him mention it. We never heard him ask for help.

Oh, no. He wouldn't, the daughter says. He never would.

So we might not know.

But I left instructions, the daughter says. I left word.

There seems to be a mix-up in that regard. Unlikely, but it happens. We might have had him confused with someone more capable. Someone else whose name begins with H.

His name is George, and I had made it very clear, the daughter says.

But you weren't with him, isn't that correct? You left word, but you weren't here.

So he hasn't been fed? He has no food? the daughter says.

Well certainly he has. He's very resourceful in most situations. We found him fending for himself.

Where did you find him? the daughter says.

I know you will laugh when I tell you where.

Tell me, then, the daughter says.

We found your father heading down the corridor, past the roll-in shower room, past the staff-only bathroom, past the office of admissions and the office of discharge, past the social worker's desk, past billing and receiving. We found him sneaking down the fire-stairs, slipping out a door marked This-Is-Not-An-Exit, knocking over a lawn chair in the garden of memories, and taking to the woods. We found your father with his creaky old boots on his feet and his old hunting hat full of moth holes on his head, with a bow in his hands and a quiver full of arrows and the yappy dog beside him, following tracks. Sniffing the air.

Sniffing the air? the daughter says. Which one of them was sniffing the air?

That remains unclear. They were somewhat obscured—somewhat hidden by the low-bent boughs and the evening mist and the interstellar haze of galactic collision where we found your father way up in the hills, in the woods where the limbs of the trees are thick and close and where the deer take the paths well marked and clear, and where the deer are old, their hoofs worn thin with running, their white tails slow to flash a warning, their eyes dark and clouded with the dust of burning stars.

We found your father waiting by the stream that flows from the jar of Aquarius, where the deer drink and rest, and the stones are cold and bright in the water. We found your father waiting, armed and ready, an arrow in his bow in the night sky to the southeast, in the constellation Orion—the celestial hunter.

I truly doubt it, the daughter says. He hardly ever went hunting. And when he did, he had a rifle. Or maybe a shotgun. I forget which.

He was perpendicular to the horizon and the celestial equator. He was hunting for his dinner.

I don't think so, the daughter says. He's a terrible shot.

He had the dog, the hunting dog. Somewhat of a help.

He never shot anything. Never caught anything.

Well, that would explain what he was eating: canned sardines with canned tomatoes.

A favorite of his, the daughter says.

He had a small fire going at the Flame Nebula, reheating his coffee.

He takes it with sugar and half-and-half, the daughter says. Though lately half-and-half is hardly allowed.

He drank it black out there in the stars. In the celestial wind. Which brings us back to the reason for our call.

But you said he was found, the daughter says. You said that my father has been found.

We are calling to inform you of the last place he was found. The very last place your father was found.

Where was he found? the daughter says.

As I have said, he turned up in places one might not expect. So I think you may laugh when I tell you where.

Tell me please, the daughter says.

We last found your father back in his bed. His eyes were closed, but he was not sleeping. His mouth was open, but he was not eating. The covers were rumpled. The pillow tossed away. The sheets soiled. The bedrails down. The window was open, and a hard wind was blowing. The curtains lifting. The little dog yapping from somewhere far off, far away. The wind saying: Shh.

Wasn't he cold with the window open? the daughter says. He must have been cold with the wind coming in.

Yes, he was, but it wasn't the wind. The wind coming in was a warm wind for spring.

I just hope he wasn't cold, the daughter says.

He was—he is—but he doesn't complain.

No, he wouldn't, the daughter says. But he doesn't tolerate the cold of late.

In that regard, we have closed the window. We have pulled the curtains. And he is here. Your father is here. Here in his bed. He is not sleeping. His mouth is open. He is not speaking.

He is waiting for your visit. Find your way. The stars are in their places. The paths between them are well marked, clear. Certain celestial objects will be recognizable.

*As we leave the skies of spring, the hunter Orion will descend into the great oceans. His dogs will follow him there, where he once lived as the son of Poseidon and where stars sometimes fall unnoticed to hiss and cool in the sea.*

*Polaris will keep steady as the pivot of the sky, no matter what the season. The celestial pole will remain nearly fixed while the stars will appear to drift nightly overhead, from east to west.*

*Betelgeuse will be visible but briefly on the western horizon soon after sunset, but by March, will find its home due south in the evening sky.*

*Dawn is now approaching. Our program is drawing to a close. With daybreak, the body of Orion diminishes in brightness as light floods the skyfield from the east. He will continue to fade until he will no longer be visible to the naked eye, having one last task before he and his retinue of stars retreat. A sole remaining star constituting the point of an arrow remains. Follow it now as he withdraws it from the quiver, as he places it in the bowstring, as he draws the bow full with the end of his strength and lets it earthward fly.*

*Sunrise is upon us. Thank you all for your kind attention.*

*If you are interested in learning more about the stars, visit our gift shop located just off the lobby. We have a variety of small souvenirs your child can carry home and a fine selection of maps of the heavens. With a little practice, anyone can locate the hunter with his bow, the star in the snout of a dog, a galaxy in a cup of water.*

*And be sure to stop at the last exhibit before you exit. We have on display our celebrated meteorite, which children particularly enjoy seeing and touching.*

*Please watch your step as you leave and as your eyes once again become accustomed to the light.*

It rests aslant, the great journeyed weight of it.

The surface burnished, darkly dinged. Smooth and cratered.

The thing is cold.

Go ahead, the father tells the child. Nothing to be afraid of.

The child leans in, past the rail: her hands across the bulk of it, the hard-pitted skin of it.

The room is warm. The thing is cold. Pocked. Smelling like a penny.

See? the father tells the child. Just what I told you: nothing to be afraid of.

Nothing at all.

# JERUSALEM

Consider the gladiolus, the mums, the marigolds along the big window. Consider the petals fallen bedside, the stems slightly bent.

The father is positioned so: knees drawn up, padded along the rail, cushioned against the bone.

Sacrum, coccyx, iliac crest: here and there the skin has gone papery thin. The daughter inspects and makes notes. "Erythema," she writes. "Induration."

Ointments have been applied. Unguents, also. There are gloves in a box and gauze in a bundle. There are places that the daughter does not like to touch: occiput, foot, lip.

Things, too, the daughter would rather not: the cup for keeping dentures wet, nail clipper, sock.

The slippers are non-skid. The pajamas are easy-care. The sheets are new and muted: sky blue, river blue, ocean.

"Nothing too bright," the father had said when the daughter inquired about colors.

"What about bone?" the daughter said. "Or buff, or even eggshell white."

"Get blues," said the father. "But nothing too soothing."

"Cornflower blue, or cerulean?"

"All right," the father said.

"Or sea?" she said.

"Or sky," the father said. "Or sky."

Consider the daughter, undaunted, steering a cart through departments.

Aisle three: outerwear, ladies shoes, hosiery.

Aisle five: housewares, cutlery, linens.

Consider the daughter, navigating the racks: white sales and displays for sleeper sets. Stopping for a comparison of colors: indigo, pewter blue, robin's egg, slate.

Sorting through pillowcases, plain and with piping. Considering thread counts.

Deciding between flat versus fitted—the father soon to be moved to a bed newly rented—now that his own bed had become unbearable.

He had slid to the foot of his old wooden bed. He slumped. No number of pillows was nearly enough. He was storm-tossed and turning. He was talking in his sleep: "Flaps! Manifold!" Or sometimes just mumbling.

His bed had become a nightly tangle, a twister of top sheets—stained and pissed on. He spilled food, capsized cups of coffee. There had been messes and mishaps and rollovers resulting in tumbles to the floor. He lay unrailed and vulnerable. All night he tugged at the covers and peeked beneath the sheets.

"What is it you're looking for?" the daughter said.

"My maps, my flight plan," he told her. "My sense of direction."

~

Consider the daughter, inquiring about sizes: twin or full for a rented bed?

Inspecting comforters and coverlets; examining the packaged stacks: a teal-blue spread, a jay-blue blanket.

Consider the daughter making her selections: mist blue, ebb tide blue; an extra light blue, an alternate dark.

Now that the new bed would soon be delivered: fully adjustable, with a gatching mattress. "Slip resistant, slide resistant," the daughter said. Electrical, inflatable.

Now that his own bed—the father's old bed—his cave of a bed, his own crumb-strewn dank den of a bed—would shortly be vacated. Surrendered. Relinquished. Gone.

"Let's go," the daughter had said, sitting beside him on his old bed—the rumpled covers, the spit on the pillow. There were crumbs of something on his chest. The pajama top was wrongly buttoned. A blanket lay askew, revealing a foot strapped in fleece, an overlong toenail snagging loose threads.

The daughter threw the covers back: waft of piss and heat. "Let's go," she said.

The father tried to sit himself up. "Where to?" he said. "Jerusalem?"

"No, not Jerusalem," the daughter said wearily. "Do you know what you're doing?"

"Returning to Zion," the father said. "I do believe I qualify."

"I do believe you've never been," the daughter said. She had him by the knees, waist. "Pivot, please," she said. "Turn this way."

"Ah," the father said. "The law of return."

"Listen," she said, "you're just relocating to the living room, remember?"

"All clear on the runway," the father said.

"Look at me," the daughter said, her face in his. "Can you see me? Do you know who I am?"

"You? You're crazy," the father said.

"Where are your glasses?" the daughter said.

"Somewhere," the father said, waving an arm to the bedside table: a hutch of stuck drawers, pulls mismatched or missing. The daughter rattled, shoved, rummaged: golf tees, pennies, cuff links, a bottle of pills spilled. There was an assortment of glasses, mainly uncased: missing lenses, taped frames. "READING", the daughter read on one, and "TV & DISTANCE" on another—what once she had written.

"There you are," she said, sliding the stems ear by ear through the sprigs of his hair.

"And there *you* are," the father said.

"You're being resituated," she said. "That's all."

"Reassigned, you mean," he said. "Called to active duty."

"Sure," the daughter said, unstrapping the fleecy pads from his feet.

"You tell them I already served. Tell them I did my time," the father said.

His feet were front and center, flat to the parquet. Old bear's feet, long and clawed. "Your slippers are where?" she said.

"Somewhere," the father said.

"Can you stand?" the daughter said with one hand to his hand, one hand to his pajama bottoms, the waistband bunched and fisted.

"Of course I can," the father said.

He stood. He wobbled. "I'm falling," said the father. She held his elbow.

"We're going down!" said the father.

"We're not," the daughter said. "Stand up straight," she said.

"Ten-hut," he said, straightening.

"Hold like this," she said, showing him how to hold her, where to put his grip. "Shift your weight," she said. "Move your butt. Left foot. Right foot," the daughter said.

"Off we go," the father said, teetering.

"Come on," the daughter said. "Step lively."

"You first," the father said.


"Out of that dark room," the daughter said as she helped him into the rented bed in the room with the big window, with the view of the river, with the sky so close and the light coming silvery through the clouds, and the last of the light of late afternoon reflected and rising from the water.

She pulled back the new sheets and punched up the pillow. "Climb in," she said, patting the new blue bedding.

The father sat. He ran his palm across the sheet.

"Like the color?" the daughter said, the daughter seeing the father with the edge of the cloth in his hands, catching it between his fingers—holding it to the light, the spill of sun: examining the stitch, hem, selvage edge.

"You didn't pay retail, did you?" the father said, lying back on the newly plumped pillow and the new blue sheets turned down and tucked in, the drape of cloth still in his old hands; the daughter seeing him there in the clear unfiltered light from the window, committing him to memory, or wanting to, at least: his head bent in solemn inspection, his hair so sparse and flinty gray, his eyes dark and deeply set, like her own, but seeming deeper still these days, but still so like her own, as he sometimes had said, at times had pointed out, but never said of late.

She folded the edge of the sheet. She pulled the blanket to his neck.

The father is situated so he can see the day nearly done. The ferry making its crossing below on the river. The flat-bottomed clouds sliding by the window.

"Cumulonimbus," the father said, his face lifted up. "Visibility fair, but fine for takeoff."

They both look past the big window: the sky above, the bare trees on the banks. Commuter train on the riverside tracks. Dining car. Faces framed in passing windows, the father recalling his train ride of long ago—scenes of soldiers furloughed home, a compartment of cadets on leave from the flight fields of the western heartlands or heading east to depots closer to the sea.

"Shipping out," the father said.

Cloud shadows on the water the color of slate. Light aslant through the big window. Lone raptor passing, talons tucked up. A squadron of geese, softly hooting: brown, buff, bone, with underbellies eggshell white.

"Heading south for the winter," the father said.

"Winter's nearly gone," the daughter said.

"Not yet," the father said as the flock banked and turned, tilting together, taken by the wind from the river.

"No," the daughter said, "not yet."

~

Consider the river.

Consider the wide and slow way of it on its way past the room with the big window, past the flowers on the sill and the father asleep in his bed—bent and bowed in his blue-sheeted bed.

Consider the hallowed and unhurried heave of the river, reflecting the sky and the fade and flow of the day; weighted with ice-shelf shards torn from its banks; the great plain plait of it, cold and in motion on the cobbled stones of its bed, sliding on between city shores against the pull of the moon sailing shrouded or unseen over city skies and sending the salty sea upstream, days from its upstate source and seep, past snow-laid fields and farms, towns and mountains, white and pure or shadowed by day, moon-blue by night; past forests or rising bluffs or broad, flinty banks where ancients knelt and chipped their blades or hunted above in the headlands and cliff lands and watched the passing of its hallowed, freighted weight; now watched still though windows by those immured in cubicles stacked above it and wanting only a view of the river—a river view—and given instead the unbidden vision of time, of passage, of the inexorable way.

Snow flies from the ledge outside the window, bright against the river. Tug and tanker. Flags and a single early sail. Unfurling the days, the finite, bright and blue winter days.

Consider the all-blue bedding the daughter has bought— the stacks of it kept on a nearby shelf. Liners and waterproof layers. Bunches of disposables resistant to odors and inadvertent leaks. Rags in a bin the daughter keeps in easy reach. Blankets and throws. Bolsters.

The daughter sizes a pillow to a case. She snaps and folds a sheet: motes fly in the shade-slatted light.

The father drifts.

"Are we loosing altitude? Are we going to ditch?" the father says.

"We're going to sleep," the daughter says.


New flowers are newly delivered. Cards bear instructions: avoid direct sun, remove old blooms, water when dry.

The daughter considers what needs to be trimmed and what needs to be kept. Much falls away unchecked: a leaf going yellow, a petiole overly bent. Petals seemingly intact go dark and discolored at a touch. Marks appear where the skin is thin and blood collects.

"Look at me, will you?" the father says, offering up an arm: leaf brown, bruise blue. "You'd think I was in some kind of fight," the father says, showing her the seep of blood from valves that leak from channels too tortuous for containment. Incompetent bone marrow. Fragile capillaries. Blood spilled. Signs of violence on a cellular level. "Hell," the father says. "You should see the other guy."

The daughter sees. She sees the wasting at his temples. She sees the trembling of his fingers, the flutter and shake of his hand when the morning sun sends the glare from the river into the big window, and he shields his eyes, hand to his brow as if in salute. His are the hands old soldiers have, the men she has seen curbside in their garrison caps, peddling the red crepe poppies, clutching them in bunches by their wire stems. Stopping motorists at traffic stops, their hands thrust into rolled-down windows. Any loose change, sir? Any amount would be appreciated. Yes, sir. Many thanks, sir—and after giving the little boy in the back seat a small but crisp salute, tottering to the curb, returning to their folding chairs and their old wounds and old stories of flights, missions, marches; of stateside training or maneuvers far afield or over rough terrain or in the air. "Tell me again," the daughter says, "about the time you were shipping out but didn't," she says. "When you lost your way over Iowa, or Ohio, or was it Oklahoma? That time," she says.

"Give me a pencil," the father says. "Let me show you where I went wrong," he says and marks down flight patterns. He draws in the cardinal points of the compass. The daughter sees the pencil pressed in his fingers; the paper aflutter, a beating wing. Fingers too knobby and flexed to be her father's fingers, hands too ragged to be her father's hands—too wrinkled and wavering. They are shreds of leaves quaking on the wintering oaks along the river, blood-brown and copper and bronze and clinging to their twigs until loosened by the wind and sent skyward across the river like loose flocks of crows and she has seen them spin and wheel and lift into the clouds all winter long, their hollow bones bearing them up, the long feathers of their wings fringed and fingered as they are lifted into the clouds on river wind, and she has seen clouds too high to be clouds, a sky too blue to be a sky, a hand too spotted and sullied to be her father's hand now grasping the bed rail and the edge of his bedsheet; a hand too worn to be the hand that once was pulling a sheet up around her shoulders, plumping her pillow—Past your bedtime, the father is saying, and he is rolling the shade down to keep out the late-setting sun of summer nights; shush now and sleep, the father says, even though it's still day, not night, no not yet, and the father explaining how the earth has a tilt, how the sun slants in summer in perigee or maybe it is apogee and the way the clocks are set and daylight is saved for some other day and some other season. He shuts the door almost shut and she hears his step on the step that creaks—the one you can't skip going down the stairs but you can going up—and she hears the hiss and sizzle of sprinklers coming on and she hears the sounds of the older children still at play in the streets, and the clatter of mower blades pushed over lawns as the smell of fresh-cut grass and wet pavement and summer rises up. And she hears the nightingale singing on the roof above the window, ready for flight.

"Here's the base, here's the takeoff," the father says. "Here's where visual checkpoints end," he says. "Farmland, the heartland," he says. "Nothing but corn—corn, corn, and more corn," and it is that summer day again with the great green seas of corn below him, the wide-flung fields of it, the shining leaves in the shimmer of heat. The sun is behind him, and he follows the shape of his traveling plane, a shadow in motion, a darker shade of green on green. Field and field flow on below him. He crosses above an unpaved road, a pickup throwing up dust. Now out ahead of him, a man on a tractor and his son beside him hear the high-away hum and they stop and squint into the sun of noonday but it is too bright for seeing, too cloudless and clear a day for looking up and then for the instant that the hawk-shaped shadow of wings and tail and fuselage pass over them and shades away the sun so they see him—yes now they see him!—see him dip his wings in what must be a hello-down-there and now the man is waving his hat and saying to his son beside him: There he goes, look there now. Now you can see him: One of our boys.

He descends. He is close enough now to see the rows, the stalks. The leaves shimmering in the heat. Tassels now. Ears. Kernels golden yellow and streamers of silk.

The daughter sits stripping stems below the waterline. Leaves wither and rot. The petals slip from their anchorings. Calyx bruised; corolla spent; blossoms with never a butterfly or bee.

There is always someone buzzing up to be buzzed in.

Four doors down, the elevator arrives with a distant ding. Someone comes thumping along the carpeted corridor. The bell is electric, droning. "Yes, I'm coming," the daughter calls. "Hold on."

"Hold here," she says, taking hold of the father by his wrist: "Hand here, foot here. Hold the rail," the daughter says, "and don't roll over."

The father peers out from the window of the train: a scattering of stars over farmland, the moon-lighted foothills, the tin-lidded lights of a small-town station. "This sleeper car," he says, on the train heading home. "There's no room to move, no room to roll over."

"I hear you," says the daughter to the buzzing at the door. "I'm here."

The daughter, at the door, puts her eye to the peephole. Beyond the lashes, floaters, and specks is a shape in a tunnel that stands and waits. The daughter squints. She is not young. She wonders about the years, the months, about the deliveries of perennials meant for transplant at a later date. She sets what comes along the ledge of window: hothouse specimens, short-lived these short sunlit days. Bulbs formerly forced, now spindly and weak with effort. Flowers freshly cut, full and showy and open, or yet unbloomed and still in bud. The daughter has been known to coax: to snip and shape, to sugar-up the cream of wheat or coffee or farina, and say, "Come on, just one more spoon, just one more sip." The daughter has been known to scold, to wheedle, to wipe a chin or dab a drip; to sniff a stem for rot, wash and scour a pot of terra-cotta gone green and mossy with a kind of sweat, or scrub clean the slime with a fisted something slid through a narrow neck. Sometimes the water is left to sit, moldering the shoots. A haze of mold forms clouds along the stalks. Sometimes the stems are hastily arranged and the stems barely reach. Water levels drop. Floral deliveries have begun to dwindle. Cards are stacked in the kitchen with the crackers and the coffee and the cream of wheat and cream of farina and the cans of beets and the borscht in a bottle and the cans of saltless soup. Hurry back. Get well soon. Thinking of you, of you.

Someone is knocking: market delivery, market delivery.

Seedless rye, creamed corn, corned beef hash, peas.

The daughter makes toast, makes coffee, cooks the cream of farina. She holds the cup and the heaping spoon.

"Ice cold," the father says.

"It's not," the daughter says.

"Always is, at this altitude," the father says.


Someone is buzzing: pharmacy, pharmacy.

Bottle, capsule, tablet, blister pack.

Directions in the smallest of print: before meals, before bed, discontinue if.

Dispense as written. Refrigerate. Keep cold.

"Cold front," the father says, skyward.

There is crazing on the window glass.

"Tower," he says, "requesting flight conditions."

Freezing rain beats on the cockpit. There is condensation on the fuselage. The propeller vibrates. The yoke starts to shake.

"Tail stall," the father says. "Let's get that nose up."

There is farmland below. Ploughed fields. Creek bed. Ice-blue lake.

Trees loom.

"Prepare for crash landing," the father calls.

Pastures rushing up. Patterns in the crops. "Extend flaps, retract landing gear," the father says. He is shearing off tree-tops, crashing down through rows of corn. He is sliding though blue cornflowers, skidding though a field of white clover.

"Am I alive or am I dreaming?" the father says.

Delphinium, marigold, forget-me-not.

Filtered light, the directions say. Fertilize in spring after the last frost. Prune back. Pinch heads.

"Pinch me, wake me," the father says. "Don't let me sleep."


Sleep has become a rattle, a bubble of spit, an upright prop of pillows.

"Breathe, please," the daughter says. She claps, percusses, auscultates: there are rhonchi in the tubes, there are wheezes in the airways. "Now, cough," the daughter says.

"Breathing or coughing?" the father says. "Make up your mind."

The daughter totes the machinery for breathing bedside—portable and motorized, designed for the delivery of mist. She cracks a vial and fills the filtered cup. She fits the transparent mask to the father's face. The hose is blue-ribbed—the solution to be dispensed for inhalation via tube and nozzle. The strap is green, stretched. The daughter tightens the fit at the father's nose and mouth. Toggle switch up, tubing unlooped. The apparatus rattles, the motor hums. The seal is tight.

"Oxygen check," the father says. "Come on, let's hear it."

There is the hush of air becoming compressed. The humming of the engine. The propeller in motion.

"It's on," the daughter says. "The air is on."

"I said, 'oxygen check!' You boys listening?" the father says.

"I can't hear you when this machine is running," the daughter says.

"We're at ten thousand feet," the father says. "Ten thousand five. Eleven thousand."

"Breathe," the daughter says.

"Top turret, waist gunners, ball turret, tail gunner," the father says. "Oxygen check."

"Shush," the daughter says. "Shush and breathe."

"Strike, wake up," the father says. "Give that turret a spin so I know you're listening."

"Who?" the daughter says.

"Not you," the father says. "Don't tie up the intercom. Shut up or keep it short and sweet."

"No talking," the daughter says. "Not now."

"Navigator, come in," the father says. "Give me a position."

"Sit up," the daughter says.

"Damn this mask," the father says, pulling at the strap. "Don't drool in the tubes, boys. You'll muck up the flow."

The daughter lifts the mask and wipes the father's mouth.

"It all freezes up at ten thousand feet."

"Here," the daughter says. "Spit."

Yellow, tan, green, brown, clear, white, pink, frothy, flecked. The daughter hates to look. "Here," she says again. "Your nose. Wipe."

Tissues, tubing, specimen cup.

Someone is knocking: special delivery, surgical supply.

"Hold the handle," the daughter says, leaving him holding the jar for piss.

Catheter, saline, adhesive remover.

Salve, gloves, hydrophilic lotion.

"Sacrum, coccyx," the daughter writes. "Erythema. Induration."

Dawn on the river. Clouds are gold or oleander or gray. The father sleeps. The daughter sits. The surface of the water is gilded and broken by a ferryboat wake.

Jacob's ladder. Morning moon. Cormorant in flight. Clouds are heaped, wooly.

The daughter adjusts the fleece around a foot. She unfolds an ear wrongly pressed.

Flowers have been slipped between the pages of a book.

Saved between the pages of a book.

Buttercup, nasturtium, coreopsis.

~

Impossible to kill, is what the daughter thinks, watering a newly delivered moon-glow gardenia. But this one is leggy, knobby at the joints, and pale where a stalk divides and turns to face the light.

Thrives on neglect, says the card recently sent with a creeping ficus. The daughter makes a space for it along the sill. Today the winter sun is dull, all glare. Downriver, the harbor is in mist. Still the river shimmers.

There are clouds above the river. There are almost always clouds above the river, even when the other skies are clear. Clouds are what the father likes to see. "Stratus," he sometimes says, when the daughter gets him unbent and sitting. "A low ceiling," he will say on certain days when the sky is an awful vault of white, and no shadows are cast.

"What's the visibility, would you say?" the daughter sometimes says, or sometimes, when there is little to say or nothing to say, the daughter will say, "And that one, there—that wisp—that one like smoke or a little bit of breath—is that a cumulonimbus?"—she will say for whatever kind of cloud it isn't.

"Sit me up," the father says, on his elbows and peering at the sky above the river. "Let me see," the father says, struggling upright on his elbows, pushing them into the bed, or gripping the rails with both of his hands.

The daughter pushes pillows behind his back.

"Higher," the father says. "Where you've got me, I just can't see. At this altitude the windshield's all fogged up."

There are curtains at the window: filmy old flows of gauze. These the daughter has unhung and laundered. "See?" she said when all was done. "Stems, tendrils: a leaf pattern under all that city grit."

Far skyline, steeple, a glass roof that slants into the sun, the distant grid of midtown streets. The train rocks along the tracks on the eastern riverbank. A dissipation of smoke. A quarried bedrock sloping to the water's edge.

The train slips between the lacework of winter trees, the river sliding beside it: ice blue or moon blue or shadows-on-the-snow blue, or the ash blue of smoke that rises from city chimneys, or the gray-blue hue of the mist that rolls some nights across an unlit road.

"Dinner," the daughter says. She heats beans, mashes potatoes. "Come on," she says, with the forkful aloft.

"You first," the father says.

"Breakfast," the daughter says. She fries eggs sunny-side and salted, or scrambled with butter beaten in. "This you'll like," the daughter says.

"I won't," the father says.

"Try it," she says.

"No," the father says. "I won't."

There is a portable pot. There is a seat for showering. The bed has a crank at the foot. The shaft—when turned—squeaks. The mattress requires tubing, hoses, alternating current. A light blinks green, blinks red. Sometimes the father awakens when it inflates, as hissy as a rubber raft.

"What is this?" he says. "Where am I? Were we forced down at sea?"

In the quiet, the daughter hears it sigh and click and watches the light. Electric cords are taped to the floor to avoid catching a foot. Sockets have reached capacity. The daughter fears the uncertain circuitry and dreams of sparks.

Light on the river. The surface ruffled.

The father's breath is in his throat—raggedy and windy as the wind that moves across the water.

Ice shards drift down with tide and flow.

The father feels the morning chill. He pulls his blanket closer. He zips his flight suit to his neck: the cockpit is cold. He is high above the river.

He is flying down the river: a chasm of light between the snowy banks and slice of cliff.

He is flying down the river: the rough-sharded cut of it, the silent and so lowly heave of it, as it hides and reappears and hides through mist and mist, moving beneath his wings and body. He checks his gyroscope, his altimeter, his air speed indicator. He reaches for the throttle, picks up speed. He climbs. He climbs. The clouds shrink away, the river now receding: a rope, a thread. He rises above the cliff edge, the cityscape, the stars. He checks his map, compares visual checkpoints: cliff, tracks, city, river. He banks and turns. The cliff face tilts. Horizon up-ended. The river emerges though the mist: shining, cerulean. Dawn spills over the edge of the sea, the endless and approaching end of the sea. The river blinds. The surface glitters. The father wakes and sees the flowers on the sill: iris, peony. He remembers where he is and blinks into the light.

There are blue-eyed asters in a glass. Bachelor's buttons in a cup. Sprigs of lavender in a tumbler.

The knob rattles. The bell is buzzing: Florist! Flower delivery.

"Hold on," the daughter says.

Someone has sent new-budded roses and a note penned in sky-blue ink.

Stems have been stripped of whatever might stick or scratch—an arrangement specifically shorn for shut-ins, for bleeders, for the easily infected. Scentless or scented enough to cover what smells and what one would rather not.

Night-blooming cereus. Sunflowers that turn their heads and follow the light. Dragons that snap.

Consider the stamens, the pistils exposed, the father lying untucked.

"Cover up," the daughter says, pulling down a new blue sheet. "I don't need to see."

There are day lilies that will not last the night. Peonies past their prime and losing their petals at a touch

Even the sprigs of fern, the foliage of gorse—even the greenery added around the rim for fill has begun to shed: tiny splinters, stiff as whiskers—what she wipes from his chin with the parts of him that have sloughed away and she finds when she cleans the razor head—electric only nowadays—now that he tends to bleed.

"Wipe," the daughter says with the same voice for swabbing oatmeal from a fissure or stink from a crease. "Wipe," whether it be a spill of milk or a ring the vase has left or a pink nose-drip or a bloody shit.

Someone sends bleeding hearts—blooms that hang like charms from a slim bower of stem; potted, with a card for care: winter in a dark place when blooms have dropped, withhold water; replant next spring in a sunny spot.

"Next spring," the daughter says.

Someone has sent a nosegay.

"Wipe," the daughter says.

Someone has sent a tussy mussy.

"This bed," the daughter says, unwinding him, releasing him from a hem of coverlet caught on toenails almost saurian—yellowed, curving, and uncut—the sort of claws a dragon would have, sought out and taunted from his cave. Enticed by a favorite food or something custardy and caloric and easy to swallow or minced or thinly sliced. "Here, try this," the daughter says, and likes to say: "It's something you like." The proffered cup: fresh-brewed coffee, with full contraband of cream and sugar. "Come on," she says. "Come on."

Lumbering forth he comes, feverish or fire breathing. The scales of his skin now motes in the blades of light when the bedclothes are shook: sheets snapped and billowing. "Cover me," the father says. "Fix me! I'm caught; I'm tucked too tight," and unsnared, he pushes away the river-blue sheets with his feet, flat and square: dragon or old bear—baited and toothless and made to dance. One foot here! One paw there! Lift your foot. Hold on. Now step!

"Grab hold," the daughter says, when she puts his hand on the bathtub bar. "Come on! Bath time," she says. "Lift your butt."

"Too cold at this altitude," the father says. "Tomorrow, maybe. I'll let you know."

"These sheets," the daughter says, tugging it from under. "What is it you do all night?"

"What do I do?" the father says. "What do you think? I'm on the town. Out getting the girls. Look at me, a man in uniform."

"Look at this," the daughter says, unwrapping him from the spiral of sheets. "You're all in tangle."

"I toss!" the father says. "I'm spinning!"

"You're not," the daughter says, putting his feet front and center, his hands on the rail. "Hand here. Foot here," the daughter says. "Look up," she says. "Get your bearings."

The father looks. There are clouds outside the window. There are clouds above them. Clouds below. Throttle. Throttle. His bed is a cockpit. The sea is below. The throttle shakes. The cockpit is cold. The parachute is packed. The hatch is locked. Radio contact is limited at best. "Tower come in!" the father calls.

"Come in," calls the daughter to the door.

The sky is the color of a storm-dark sea. The starlight is growing dim and distant.

"Navigator," says the father. "Give me your check points. Correct for drift."

Someone at the door, rattling and tapping: Delivery of flowers! Signature required.

"Weather ahead," the father says. "Change course, navigator. Altitude check."

Shards on the river. Ice on the wings.

"We're in it now," the father says. "Ailerons, ailerons. Co-ordinated rudder."

The nose dips. Airstream noise increasing. Now in a spin, a downward spiral. Tachometer past telling. The airspeed indicator needle stuck, set, pegged to last red lines.

"Wings level," the father says. "Ease up on the nose."

Eight thousand, seven thousand, six thousand feet.

The father descends.

His bed is below him, waiting on the water—a life raft of rubber among the shards of ice that glow moonlight-blue in the stone-dark sea. He feels the wind of descent. He hears the hum of the fall becoming a buzz, becoming a whistle, the pitch increasing. Five thousand, four thousand, three thousand feet.

"Full rudder! Come on!" the father says.

"Coming," says the daughter at the door—the daughter signing and receiving.

"Ailerons in neutral," the father says. The wings go level. The nose comes up. The river falls away. The boats grow small, smaller. The life raft is receding, unneeded. The bed is disappearing. Five thousand feet. Six thousand. Seven. Gaining altitude. Pulling up.

The father looks down at the thread of the river. He is warm in his flying suit, fleece-lined, zipped to the neck.

The air is clear. The stars grow closer. The Milky Way is a mist of stars, a field of white clover.

Aster, moonflower.

There are flowers still left along the sill: withered leaves of strawflower, fallen shreds of pearly everlasting.

Consider the heads that nod and lean to the lip of the vase: jonquil, bergamot, coreopsis.

Consider the father with his head on the pillow and his hair astray like the wisps of clouds that fly in front of the moon.

There are clouds around the cockpit. "Altostratus?" asks the daughter.

"Never at this elevation," says the father.

There are fingers of mist along the window. Snow spins down from the edge of the cliff face

"Banking right," the father says, turning now above the river. "Come on," he tells the daughter.

"You first," he hears her say.

The clouds disperse. Visibility is unlimited. The water below him is as clear as the air. The stones in the riverbed are set in their places, smooth and cool in the earth of the riverbed: slate blue, cinder black, buff, bone.

Consider the daughter at the door with her arms full of flowers: gladiolus, mums, calla lilies.

Consider the father far past her as he heads downriver. The dip of a wing. Dreams ceasing.

He hurtles down the corridor of water, the dusk-blue sea is tilting ahead of him, in his sights—approaching and unreachable—becoming an alternate dark.

# DETAILS OF GRIEF

It is not quite spring. The threshold—yes, but not yet the frantic tug and sweet hum and tweak of life. Some birds of the past season still live, still hold on. Winter doves amble amid the rows of stones. Geese going over take a wide turn seeking early open water or patches where the snow has been cleared for digging. Crows watch from steeples. Starlings sit along chimney rims in the shimmer of forced heat. Trees are still bare of leaves, but come dusk, the silhouettes of limbs are dressed in clusters of clouds the color of sundown and smoke. There is wind. Twigs click. Paper blows in the road. Hats tumble and bounce away on their brims. Old letters held in the hands rattle; as the grip loosens and weakens, they are torn away. (Hello to all and how's the weather out by you? Holding up here. Home soon.) The pages—flimsy with the years—take flight. There is no holding on.

Far away in the heartland, great sweeps of snow still blow above the fields. The slender thoroughfares of mice and voles are drifted over. Old furrows are marked only by stubble and shadow. Implements of tillage are stowed. Plows wait.

But in certain fields, it is not too soon for making holes and digging shapes that hold long boards and wooden walls. In any season there are places in the earth where the earth is up-turned, broken by pickaxe, lifted by backhoe. A man rides inside the glassed-in cab and engages the gears. The metal neck creaks and grinds at the joint, then extends and drops the jaw-hinged scoop. The teeth scrape into the frozen sod. Plates of shale are cracked and rise, trembling. Earth is lifted. The soil, powdery and crystalled, drips from the teeth, as if it be some old dragon forced in famine to eat the very earth, oh mouthfuls soon enough when the final wooden walls collapse. The neck and scoop swings clear. Old stones scoured smooth by long-gone glacial ice are split or tossed intact. What rises from the hole is the cold smell of iron and ice and sweet split root.

More men come. They carry shovels and spades. They step on the clods of earth and the torn-up rags of turf as they walk over dates and names cut into flat-laid stones. Over here, Bill, one says. We're two rows over.

A road winds though the field of stones, past the plastic blooms stuck in on wire stems, past a few folk dressed in clothes for cold spring days. Men in suits. Women in their coats and hats. Cars come and go, headlighted despite the brightness of day, and some long-bedded for bearing their consignments of newly-boxed bones behind the curtained windows. Those who await their spaces in the earth. There is no hurry. New holes have been made among the older specimens supine in their quarters in poses of comfort and repose—an arrangement of limbs, of hands placed just so; the oldest of these are held in place not by sinews yet unsnapped or cured flesh but by de-composing clothes and the narrow span of boards.

Early light. Oh yes: the living stir. Still abed, their night-time cries of remorse, grief, regret subside. Dread of the final dark dissipated. Dreams pushed away. They breathe the morning air, remember where they are. Drapes are parted. Shades are rolled up. They view their desiccated lawns and the salt stains on the flagstone; newspapers delivered to the shrubbery. A father reads the front pages, the sports pages, the obituary lists. A father wipes the fog from a mirror with the edge of his backhand, lathers up. A mother sweeps, wipes crumbs from a table. A boy slams a door. A daughter opens a book of poems and finds there the crumbling flowers she had pressed. Infants kick off their covers. Last year's leaves and twigs from winter storms clot in the gutter traps. Children tumble from rooftops. A hawk in flight folds her wings against herself and falls from the sky, drops upon the back of a resting dove, presses her claws though its feathers and into its skin and ribs and lungs. Loose feathers fly away. Vessels are pierced. Blood fills its mouth. The open beak. Struggles cease. The body is opened. A page of the old letter taken up by a gust is blown flat against a kitchen window. A woman standing at her sink and doing dishes looks up and reads: Dear George, where are you and whom do you think you're fooling?

The men climb down into the rough-dug hole. Tree roots protrude, some thick as rope, some delicately divided as lace. Here and there, shards protrude from the earth wall: a piece of crockery (blue willow woman with umbrella), a base of amber glass (beer bottle, tossed away by a grave digger himself long-ago subterranean), a fracture of flint (undulled by the days, the so many days), smooth stones the color of blood and the color of bread. A pebble of quartz, opaquely white as a tooth.

The men stand in the hole and cut the tree roots with their sharpened spades. They make the earth walls flat and plumb with their shovels. Sprays of soil fly as the shovel blades flash and dip above the rim.

The men set the boards. They swing their sledgehammers to the struts. The struts sink. The boards shake. Soil sifts through the slats. The earth walls are shorn up.

The anteroom is opened. The doors are a pair, sliding apart with the sound of a low rumble, a rattle of bearings along the metal track. The daughter is reminded of a trip she took as a child, some long-ago travel on train or scenic trolley or some other vehicle in motion, moving away. Even opened, the room is dim. A switch is flicked; a fixture overhead blinks and lights a showroom of sorts—an exhibit of carpentry, an assortment of woods. A selection of solids is arranged in a row. This poplar, this birch, this oak, this maple. Grain and whorl. Luster. Here, a separate aisle of veneers: of cypress and yew. Of mahogany, black and deep as a tarn. Here, a display of products only pine, of boards simply sanded, left unfinished.

The lids that lift are propped. The quarters are close. Interiors are displayed. All lacking decoration, ornament, or trim. Fabric therein arranged in a symmetry of folds and small drifts. Padding. Pillows appear to have been plumped.

A dearth of excess pervades.

A woman—the daughter—walks among these unadorned accommodations. She appears somewhat worn and disinclined to hurry. Decisions must be made in the details of grief. She carries a parcel, papered and twined, held under her arm, tucked. A bundle of some bulk. She looks for a place it can be put. She looks for a window, some aperture that allows in natural light.

Allow me, says the skull-capped proprietor, the purveyor of boxes. He extends his hand to take the bundle. The clothing? he asks, the jacket and such? he says, taking it in his fingers by the closure of the twine, setting it down on a surface that appears to be teak. Or perhaps it is a fir, a species of evergreen wood.

Birch is a good choice, says the purveyor of boxes. This one is the Elijah, displayed in birch. Also available in mahogany or beech. As is the Homewood. And the Sinai. Or, if you prefer, we have each in oak.

Solid or veneer. Both. Hence the difference in price.

Also the David, the Emmanuel, the Mount Olive, he says. A Star of David on the lid would be purely optional. Though a lack of decoration of any kind is more in keeping.

The daughter is moving through the room. She slides her hand along the wood. Her hands seem older than she is and older that what has been hewn.

She looks for where a box such as this may be opened, so fine the carpentry is, and given how the top slopes keenly to the body of it and how fitted is the lid. Allow me, says the purveyor of boxes, moving beside her, standing close by, close in. A nudge so slight to have her step aside. Not quite a push, no not nearly so. He puts his hands on a panel that is meant to slide away. The lid is the kind that moves to expose the face, the head, the place that the face and the head would be. The purveyor of boxes pulls the part along the groove. A slide of cabinetry, the sound of wood on wood.

The Mount Olive interior, he states, is available in a variety of colors.

The daughter walks from box to box, the insides of which appear variations only of white.

Including, he says, eggshell and ivory, both of which are very popular these days. However, he says, if you prefer something more traditional, I'd suggest the paler parchment or even the bone.

Or this, says the purveyor of boxes, now beside a box of a wood-whorled gold, with what seems to be a light from within the grain, and reminiscent of burl, but without the knots.

Or, he says, we have this one done in candlelight—as you can see it's somewhat darker than the shade we call seashell or even mist.

The daughter looks into the box. The fabric is gathered into tufts. The edges are sewn in a series of folds. The pillow is placed as it would be in a bed but this is not a bed. This clean bright box is nothing like the bed where the father had slept and waked and took hold of the rails and held on and held on where he lay in the damp on the stains and the spills and the crumbs and the sometime smell of piss and sweat. Inside this box of gold-whorled wood is a whiteness that is not ivory or candlelight or mist, but a whiteness the color of a soft-boiled egg getting cold in a cup; the color of potatoes that the daughter mashed up and scooped on a spoon and lifted to his mouth: come on, just a little, just one more bite. The color of pudding in a bowl in his lap: go on, it's good, take a taste. Or tapioca with cream on the table at his bedside, left untouched in his dish.

The daughter appears to be pale. A lightness of the head, a dryness of the mouth.

As I mentioned before, says the purveyor of boxes, we have an assortment of shades. We can mix and match, he says, noting her glassiness of eye and taking her blank look as indecision.

The Eternal is available with a Zion lining. Also the Jerusalem, if you would like to take a look.

He two-handedly lifts. A perceptible creak.

The purveyor of boxes explaining the lack of brass or bronze or handles or grips. No bolts on a lid, he says. No hinges employed. No nails. Instead the necessity of pegs, of dowels— and a sturdy glue in strategic spots. I can assure you, he says, that nothing you see here was built on the Sabbath.

Strict adherence to custom, he says. No metals of any kind employed. And certainly, he says, no rings on the fingers. No medallions, belt buckles or such.

The volume of his voice lifts, as if to instruct. Nothing permitted, he says, that would not readily return to the earth.

The purveyor of boxes steps forward with some haste and lowers a lid. It appears as if his fingers will be pinched, but he seems to know some special way to grip.

Which brings to light the problem of the clothing, he says. Clothing in general, he says, and in this case, the matter of the jacket.

The purveyor of boxes takes the package from where it has been set. He fusses with the twine. A knot. The paper is torn away.

Ah yes, he says, the problem of the jacket. Not the jacket per se, he says, but the issue of the zipper. The tendency to decompose being preferable. Because such a thing as this, such a thing as a zipper—would not.

Not what? the daughter says.

The zipper aside, and in regards to the jacket, such as it is, says the purveyor of boxes. It is not quite in keeping, he says, owing to its condition. See for yourself, says the purveyor of boxes, his hands on the jacket, his hands turning it open and partially inside out. The lining is quite tattered, he says. His hands on the neck of it, the frayed flap of a pocket. The worn cuff and collar. The leather there showing rot.

His flight jacket, the daughter says. It's very old.

Nonetheless, says the purveyor of boxes. A simple shroud is certainly more the custom. Certainly more in keeping. We have both cotton and linen in stock.

Was your father at all observant? asks the purveyor of boxes.

Observant? says the daughter.

A practicing Jew, he inquires. Was he observant of custom, or high holy days?

Observant? says the daughter. Observant, yes—of a cover of clouds, or ice on the wing, or the shadow of his plane over snow-covered hills; observant of the high holy days of smoke and wind and the sway of trees at the end of a runway; of the direction of dust blowing on a desert road or the formation of a front.

The daughter leans against the Elijah.

The purveyor of boxes taps the veneer of the Homeward with his finger, a gesture practiced, subtle, of patience wearing thin.

Worn in the war, is that it? says the purveyor of boxes. Or some sort of special request?

~

The shovels fly from the hole, then the spades. Whoa, Bill! calls the man up in the backhoe. Watch what you're doing, would you? Look where you're throwing that stuff.

Get on over here, calls the man in the hole to the one in the backhoe. Get on out of that thing and give us a hand up.

~

The daughter stands beside the box. Which wood? she wonders. Then remembers: birch, yes—that was it. All right, she had said to the purveyor of boxes. This one—the birch. Yes.

She wonders if there is space enough at the shoulders. She wonders if outside the clouds are still low and tightly layered.

She wonders if the pillow in the box had been fluffed enough to give the father's head the right tilt: not too extended at the neck, and his chin and jaw not too tucked. And if someone tried to put his dentures in his mouth when his jaw was stiff. Of if they had been slipped in without force or mess or fuss when his mouth had gone slack. And if someone had wiped the spit from his face the way she would have wiped it. And if someone had put his hands in place with the sleeve and cuff of the jacket pulled down to the wrist.

She wonders if the room where he had been kept was a room kept as cold as a day might be when snow was coming. And if, outside, the clouds coming in are cirrus. Or cumulonimbus. Or if it has gotten colder. Or if there is much wind.

She wonders if the jacket still fits, and then thinks: it does, it must; there had been the loss of weight.

She wonders if there are other kinds of cold. Climes unknown.

If there are weathers in the earth.

She places her hands along the lid, to get a grip to get it open.

To see if the jacket has been properly zipped.

# BADLY RAISED
# AND TALKING WITH THE RABBI

This? I've had this for years.

No, not black. More of a charcoal.

Not that black is even necessary nowadays.

Dark colors, on the conservative side, isn't that what they say?

Anyway, there just wasn't time to shop.

She was hell-bent on getting him in the ground today.

The daughter, that's who.

I had absolutely nothing to say about it.

Why she decided to do the whole Jewish thing is beyond me.

I mean, George just wasn't that observant.

No waiting, no flowers. And no viewing either.

Who'd want to anyway? He was very bad toward the end.

He wouldn't walk. He wouldn't eat.

He just lay in that bed in the middle of the living room.

You heard me: the living room.

Can you imagine?

Oh, so inconvenient! How could I have people over?

What was I supposed to do—serve drinks sitting around a
hospital bed?

That's right. The one she rented. With those bars or rails or whatever you call them.

All her idea. Don't get me started.

She was into everything. Right up to the end.

His heart, she said. Or a clot, or not enough clotting. Something. She wasn't clear.

Of course I asked. But she's barely civil.

Just not a very nice person.

Look. Over there. There she is. That's her.

Oh, she's older than that. She dyes her hair.

Go ahead if you have to. I don't mind. Condolences or hello or whatever. I don't care.

You, did? When was this? So you see what I mean. Nothing but trouble.

She's that way with everyone. Very intense.

It's like I told her when she'd stop in to see him: Take it easy, why don't you?

She was always barging in. What could I do? The front desk let her up.

And of course she had a key. She had a hand in everything.

All the medications, all the food, all the bills.

She took his car away, you know. Oh yes! Sold it right out from under him.

I told her: You're taking away his dignity. You're taking away his independence.

That's what I said.

Did she expect me to schlep him all over?

Not that he got out much, not this past year anyway.

Doctors appointments. Sometimes he just liked to go for a drive.

But that was all over when she took away the car.

She managed to destroy any shred of enjoyment he had left.

Even the food, when she started in on that. You should have seen her.

She poured out the borsht. She threw out the Ritz. The cantaloupe. The lox.

She completely emptied out the freezer.

Well it happened to be *my* rocky road, *my* coco-mocha— not his.

She didn't even bother to ask.

Excuse me, Barbara, but is this your ice cream? That's all she had to say.

Common courtesy.

But no. Everything went in the trash.

Too much potassium. Too much salt. Too much this or that.

Oh, please. No, it wasn't the doctor. She did this all on her own.

That's just how she is. Rude. Offensive. Badly raised.

Now look. See that? Now she's talking to the rabbi.

Trust me: No one can stand her. He's just being polite.

Oh, he's wonderful. He's very popular. Very modern, very reformed.

He was at Beth El on the Palisades, but they lured him over to El Emanuel.

Oh, yes—a much more upscale community.

And he's a terrific speaker.

I happen to know that he gets five hundred for funerals.

But you'll see. He's very charismatic.

He packs them in. And not just for the High Holy Days
either.

Any Shabbat, you can't get a seat.

And Rosh Hashanah's completely sold out.

But go ahead. Ask him. After. Why not?

You still might get in for Yom Kippur.

# INSCRIPTION

## HE NEGLECTED THE HEDGES, BUT HE CALLED HOME ABOUT CLOUDS

Can't do it, says the man who letters stone. Too long. Can't be done.

They stand in a yard full of stones—an assortment of rough-cut and polished rock; a display of styles of chiseling, of ways of engraving dates and names. The man has a chisel. The man has a hammer.

And what is this anyway? says the man who letters stones. Hedges, clouds? What is this about?

Just make it fit, the daughter says. Make the letters smaller.

No space for the name, no space for the dates. It won't work, I tell you. All wrong. Won't fit.

Skip the dates, the daughter tells him. Just do the words—that's all I want.

There's too many words, says the man who letters stone. Can't go smaller. Can't go chipping away willy-nilly. There's fracture, there's fault. It's the nature of the rock.

The daughter looks at the nature of the rock—the marble, the blocks of granite, the limestone and basalt. Some are nearly as white as cumulonimbus. Some gray as stratus. Some the color of the undersides of thunderheads, near black and shot with bits of mica that glint like stars or lightning spark. And some are as dark as a night without stars to mark the start of nights that will come unnumbered; nights without dates, nights without days, nights that will be—will always be—nothing like the night.

What exactly is it that you're trying to do? says the man who letters stones with the hammer in his hand.

# THE RHYTHM OF DIGGING

The shovels rise and dip. The soil is flung. Wind takes away
the dust. What is lifted out to make a space becomes a mound
on the grass where the grass has been trampled flat. Clod, pebble, soil, shard, pieces of root, pieces of rock. There is a stone
on the heap.

The daughter is grown and growing older. She was once a
daughter who liked clouds made of cotton. She was once a girl
who kept stones on a shelf.

The father once was a father who called home about
clouds. He was hardly home, but he carried home stones.

There are sounds in the hole: the singular scrape and grate
as the walls are made, the steady slide of metal against stone,
the huff of the men as they breathe and work.

The daughter watches the arc of flying earth and the up-
and-down swing of their shovel blades.

Clod, pebble, soil, shard, pieces of root, pieces of rock.

The daughter will wait until the men are done with their
digging. The stone will be smooth and heavy in her hand. It will
fit in her pocket. It will be as cold as the day is, as the very earth.

# THERE'S NOTHING HERE YOU'D WANT

Broom clean, the realtor had said. Don't give the buyer a reason to renege.

Certainly not. Not after so many delays: the dickering over price, the demands for repairs before the closing date.

One last look, the daughter decided, arriving with broom in hand for a final sweep.

By now, of course, cabinets had been cleared. Belongings had been sorted. Discards had been bagged and stuffed down the garbage chute. Even the doorway mezuzah had been removed, although the father's name remained in place, under the bell for buzzing in, below the hole for peeping out.

Closets had been emptied. Clothing bundled up. Personal effects dispersed.

Furniture, furnishings, father.

Early on the daughter had surveyed the wreckage—the old foldout sofa, the bulky end tables, the banged-up dining room set. She decided what items she could carry, and what would require vans and men—including the hospital bed where the father spent his days and nights, and the bedroom bed where he once had slept.

Early on she noted what would require packing up and hauling out—including the father's live-in girlfriend and her well-stocked cupboard of comestibles.

The woman—Babsie—had hinted at her impending departure.

Where do we sit? Where do we eat? she had said as the father's pill bottles piled up on countertops and collected on the kitchen dinette, and as the sofa became stacked with plastic bins that held mattress pads, pajamas, changes of bedding. The chair with a toilet seat and built-in bucket was positioned bedside; the urinal was kept at the ready, plainly displayed.

Personal care items, the daughter said.

Poop pan, the father said. Piss pot.

It's more like a sick room or a hospital ward, said Babsie while she polished off a dish of *kugel*. This is much more than I bargained for.

The daughter rolled up the rug. Pile and fringe, the potential for damage: the father could slip; his shoes could catch.

Obstacles were everywhere. The father could stumble. A hazard, the daughter said, shoving aside the clutter.

She relocated lamps, secured electrical cords with tape. She plugged in night-lights that glowed like miniature moons.

The credenza was relegated to a corner. Dining room chairs were dismantled. The glass-topped coffee table—an item nearly invisible and subsequently hazardous—was summarily displaced.

All my nice things, said Babsie between bagel bites. It's hardly my home any more.

Never was, the daughter said.

Nevertheless, the father took a spill.

I'm fine, fine, he said, sprawled on the kitchen floor. He waved them away. Stop making a fuss, he said. Just give me a minute to sit.

The daughter knelt beside him. Just what did you think you were doing? she said. Just tell me what you were trying to do.

Boil a hot dog, the father said with great sorrow. Heat up some beans.

Well, said the daughter, that's that. New rules, she said. New footwear. Supervision.

She sorted through his shoes—the slippery soles, the dangerous laces—and bundled them up with his clothes to give away—the trousers gone too loose, the shirts he couldn't button.

He took to staying in the bed where she put him beside the big window. He pushed her away when she pulled at his arms to have him stand. I can't! Can't you see that? the father said.

Come on, the daughter said. Get going. Just a few little steps.

Enough! the father said.

My golden years—ruined, Babsie said.


The radiator had rust. Grout was crumbling.

A tough sell, the realtor told them.

Inadequate upkeep, or the total lack, took its toll. Offers were not pouring in. Hardly a nibble, the realtor said. The kitchen was obsolete and downright dangerous. The oven overheated. A back burner shot stars. Nothing had ever been replaced. No need, the daughter told the realtor: Babsie did not cook, though the shelves were stocked for snacking. Actual meals consisted of dining out or ordering in. Hence the out-of-date kitchen and its old appliances, the realtor explained to potential buyers. Hence the price.

The bathroom, too, was a liability. Buyers want tiles in muted tones, the realtor said, and showerheads with adjustable functions—forceful massage or sprinkle of rain. They want self-heating towel racks, not safety-grip bars screwed into the wall. Not toilets with handicap seats.

Inquiries were made about the crack inside the tub. Purely cosmetic, the realtor explained to interested parties, defending his contracted turf. Nothing structural, he explained when they asked him: Were any of the occupants somewhat obese?

You never know when a buyer might come by, the realtor told the daughter, so keep the place clean. And by the way, maybe you could paint.

The daughter mopped, wiped, swept.

Babsie cleaned her plate.

The father wasted away.

Babsie let nothing go to waste.

Perfectly good cake, she said with fork in hand, picking through leftovers the father had left.

I never liked cake, the father said. Rugelach—maybe.

Tapioca then, the daughter said. I added eggs. Lots of pro-tein.

Fish eyes, the father said. Forget it.

How about a blintz? Sour cream or blueberry? How about a nice potato knish?

Three strikes, said the father. How about that?

His hand shook. A tremor of utensils. The shakes, the father said. I'm missing my mouth.

The doctor was kindly, his voice soft.

Try adaptive devices, the doctor said. Spoons with big grips. Sectional plates.

He's gotten so weak he can hardly sit up, the daughter told him.

Have you considered getting some help? he said. Live-in? Round-the-clock?

A woman—Bettylou—was subsequently hired; someone bigger than Babsie and primarily toothless, but having Babsie's potential for consumption. The father listened as they made meal selections—Babsie and Bettylou commiserating over menus: Nine Napkin Burger. Peking Palace. Hot Wings.

This sounds good, said Babsie, contemplating an order of barbequed meat. Want to split a bucket of ribs?

Big meals were telephoned in.

The father struggled to turn in his bed. Need help? asked Bettylou as she speared a wing. Looks like you're trying to roll yourself over.

Sure, said the father, but you go ahead. Finish eating. Relax. No rush.

The doorman announced impending deliveries. Pizza! he called. On its way up!

Bettylou folded over her slice of pepperoni. I'd offer, she said, but it's loaded with salt.

Looks good, the father said.

And I don't think it's Kosher, said Bettylou.

Cheese stretched. Sauce dripped. No, she said, definitely not.

~

Bettylou did less, ate more. Chips, dips, assorted nuts. She requested a pay raise. The daughter shelled out. She requested another. The daughter acquiesced. Suspicions were aroused when valuables disappeared: a watch, a ring, and a tub of butter. Voices were raised. Fingers were pointed. Ugly scenes ensued: Who polished off the nachos? Who paid for the butter pecan? Inevitably came the shakedown: She would leave them in the lurch if they didn't cough up. I'm walking, said Bettylou when she walked off the job. Jews, she said.

The doctor called, concerned and gently inquiring.

He's losing weight, the daughter told him. He just won't eat.

Forget the low salt, the doctor said. Give up the restrictions. Give him whatever he likes.

And I like him, said the father. He's a snappy dresser. Very coordinated. Nice ties. Think he'd like a few of mine?

The daughter rummaged through closets and cabinets, explored the rooms where the father wasn't. The dresser drawers groaned as they opened, the closet doors rattled on their runners. What's going on in there? the father called from his living room bed. What are you looking for?

Just re-organizing, she called. Straightening up.

Don't bother, the father said. Leave it be.

He raised up on his elbows and peered over the bedrail when she toted in items largely inconsequential: a bottle of expired borsht, a box of stale *matzoh*, old combs, pens with dried-up ink.

See? the daughter said. There's nothing here you'd want.

A cookie sheet was displayed, sticky with disuse and old grease. What about this? the daughter said.

Hers, the father said.

Babsie's, the daughter said. Sure. But does she use it? I mean, does she bake?

Are you kidding me? the father said. Are you nuts?

She dragged old golf trophies and his bag of clubs bedside. Bits of dry grass clung to the woods; there was rust on the putter.

Mine, the father said. And that nine-iron is new.

Let's get rid of what you're not using, she said.

There's nothing I'm not, the father said.


The doctor called, asking about progress.

None, the daughter said. Not one bit.

Have you thought about moving him out? the doctor said. Alternative care? Long term?

Forget it, said the father. I'm fine where I am. Don't try and pack me up with the rest of the crap. No need to cart me out.

Despite the signs, departure had been sudden. Strength ebbed. A weakness of the limbs. A pallor. The skin was fragile, thinned, and prone to shear and tear by the very sheets.

Breakdown was imminent, but never occurred. There were no tears, no hugs, no note of taking leave.

Speaking of funerals, the father had said

Who is? said the daughter.

There's a plot—all paid for, he said. There are papers packed away but I'm not sure where.

No need, she said.

Listen, he said, I am stuck in this bed. It doesn't appear that I'm getting up.

Not true, said the daughter. You just need more time and a little more rest.

He sat himself up off the pillow and reached through the rail. He grabbed for her hand. Listen, he said. Nothing fancy. No flowers. A song might be nice. One of my favorites.

Which one?—just in case, the daughter said.

You pick, he said.

Daddy, the daughter said.


Babsie dusted off her suitcases and began to gather up her menus.

The realtor suggested that the daughter relent. Drop the price, he said. A seller's market—or was it a buyer's? Something to that effect. The daughter never quite understood.

The realtor re-strategized. The sale was re-pitched: must-see, spacious, motivated seller. The kitchen and bathroom were retro, not dated. The rooms were roomy. The safety of a door-man building was emphasized. As was the terrace and the living room window with sweeping views of the city and the river. As was permission for apartment-type pets: well-behaved cats, dogs of a specified weight, birds if kept caged and not prone to squawk.

Babsie soon abandoned the nest. She snacked, packed, and flew the coop.


Broom clean, the realtor had said. Take a broom and tidy up.

The daughter here at the door for final check.

She puts her key into the lock.

Somewhere else, in other rooms, a radio plays. The elevator ding at the end of the hall. Somewhere trash rumbles down a chute.

She turns the key and puts her shoulder to the door. It sticks a bit. It always did.

Inside the sense of vacancy pervades, the feeling of a place sealed up. The air is still, the windows tightly shut. The walls are bright with late-day sun and sunlight off the river.

She walks room to room, aware of her footfall on the parquet floors and the echo of an empty space.

Entranceway, living room, bedroom, kitchen.

She checks under the sink. She opens closet doors. Here and there are items left behind: a single glove, a folded sheet. She finds that the cabinets are clean and empty, except for a box of crackers left on a shelf. Babsie's?—the daughter wonders—or maybe the woman formerly employed?—and she bags it up. She finds a thin bar of soap in the tub. And there's a rag behind the bathroom door. Small things, here and there. Left behind. Left in place.

She takes the broom and the pan and starts to sweep. Into the corners. Under the radiators. Along the molding.

She pokes her fingers through the little pile of what has been gathered up. She sifts through the grit: a match, a Roosevelt dime, a capsule, a pill. Chips of paint.

There is nothing left, nothing more to do or keep her. Broom clean and done. She must get on now. Papers must be signed. Keys must be handed over. Come on, she says out loud. Get going.

She gathers up the bag of discards: towels, glove, rag, old food, sweepings. She drags it down the corridor of doors to the one just midway down—the door left always unlocked, without a name or bell or hole for peeping out.

The room is narrow. The walls are windowless. What no one wants has newly accumulated: a stack of crockery, newspapers tied with twine, a flowerpot of earth.

She lifts the bag to the mouth of the chute. It is not heavy. There wasn't much.

She pushes it in and lets it fall. It shudders along the narrow walls, thudding down the sides of the shaft.

What rises is the faint smell of rot, a ghostly rush of wind, and the silence of descent.

# IN THIS LAST SLIPPING-PAST YEAR

Uneven strands, the roughness of stubble—the father's appearance had become one of dishevelment and neglect. This look of the unkempt, the daughter decided, simply would not do. In this the year of the faltering father—of a man in disarray—the father was continually in a mess: pillow askew and damp with drool or sweat or spill, his hair a silvery wisp at his forehead and pressed flat at the occiput. She saw the shadowy dent of his jaw, his unshaven cheek and chin. A tidying up was definitely in order—a haircut, she said, or at least a trim. (Did he know how overgrown it had become, how derelict?)

Essential implements had since been collected and kept in a little tote—a satchel, as the father called it, that the daughter had too often packed and carried: toothbrush, comb, denture cup—necessities for a hospital stay in case the need arose for an overnight, for those times the doctor emerged from the curtained cubicle to recommend an extra day for observation or to repeat the usual better-safe-than-sorry speech. A short stay in the hospital for tests, for a tune-up—that's how it was put. A few days, a few nights, at most.

(Did he not tire of the mechanical bed and of the button he had to press for help? Did he grow weary of the nurses' voices from a speaker in the wall, the odd electronic lilt: Can we help you? Did you call? Are you comfortable?

I make a living—that's what he said to that—always said to that—an answer largely misunderstood and lost on most.

A living? they said. Why, Honey, sure you do! And they went their way, passing pills and filling pitchers. Pushing off the call button. Snapping off the light.)

The satchel sat bedside, bulging as items were added over time: comb, safety razor, aftershave. And then for the inevitable, for longer stays: foldable slippers, a dollar or two for sundries—the morning paper, a pen or pencil, a stick of gum—and should the father need a trim, there were scissors for snipping stray strands and the little soft-bristled duster for whisking away the clipped bits that get stuck in the creases. Get busy, she said, handing the father the comb—this look of the unattended not at all in keeping with what she would generally permit.

But she had, as the saying goes and as she herself had said—let things slide somewhat in this past year—this year of well-worn hope and a father nearly worn out. In this the year of the machine for wheezes, this year of the wavering gait and of falls nicely foiled—for the most part—by strategically placed furniture in this year of a fear of falling, a fear of walking—and finally, oh yes: a fear of simply standing still—there were attempts at steadying by clutching a wobbly table or unstable chair, resulting in a shaking at the knees, a strange stiff buckling of sorts, and finally his whoa! whoa! as he went slowly, thrashingly crashing down.

In this last slipping-past year of the banishment of rugs that scatter, this year of footwear solely rubber-soled and tread-ed, in this slow and steady slide of a year from footed cane to walker to wheelchair to bed, the daughter often found the father where he lay in the ambush of his bedclothes, snared by a twist of top sheet, undone by unsnapped pajama bottoms. In this year of decline and mechanical beds, the father had gone from keeping up appearances to keeping up the side-rails, of holding tight to the bars to stop the drag of gravity that settled him toward the foot, of holding his hands tight to his chest, arms elbow-bent: Come on, she said. Straighten out, stretch stretch stretch or you'll be folded up for good. (Was he not sick to death of the threats? Of needing to nod and agree? Did he not want her to just shut up?)

One step forward, two steps back, the father said in this the year of daughterly reassurances, of what the daughter called the process of a slow recovery, this year of mishaps she called minor setbacks as the father had gone from sport coats and din-ners out to disposable diapers and pajama tops. From break-fasts of smoked and salted fish to cheating on a diet deemed low-sodium-mechanical-soft. (Didn't he tell that dietician to take a hike?) In this the year of the trembling hand there was the trouble with spoons and forks and spillage and clods of day-old egg amidst the bedclothes. Coffee sloshed. Food was scraped and pushed along the plate, the father seizing the spoon shovel-wise and fisted as a prisoner would at mess.

I'd kill for a slice of pizza, the father said, and so they struck out. A treat, the daughter said. The father was assisted from his bed—lifted, if truth be told, and taken to stand on the cold tiles, toileted there and wiped clean in the places beyond his reach. (Did he mind the daughter seeing what she saw? Did he mind it when a doctor told him: I guess your daughter's seen it all.) Then well washed as he held fast to the bathroom sink— showers being recently being abandoned: the lack of footing, the inability to lift a leg above the level of the rim, the potential for a scald. (Did he miss the unchecked fall of water on the body? Had he forgotten the feel of being clean?) The father was outfitted in non-slip shoes and snap-closed shirt and pull-up pants. She stepped back as if to survey. Hair stuck out above his ears, all around unruly. You need a trim, she told him.

We'll see, he said.

Then comb at least, she said. And he made the part and pulled it through the way he had always done, smoothing with his other hand as he always had done, as she knew he would do; that at least remained. A few more things, she said, just let me check. This collar is turned in. This sock has slightly slipped. This cuff is too tight. He lifted a foot, a hand; he turned his head. There, the daughter said, making an unnecessary adjustment, heeding to the smallest of details: from the belaboring of buttons, the security of shoelaces, the milliliters in a cup of coffee, the milligrams of salt in a slice of bread, the swallowing the last bit left on the dinner plate—to the setting of his wristwatch to the minute and the winding of its workings, while leaving untouched the inexorable slide of time and time left between the clock ticks of what must be must be must be.

There, she said. No worse for wear.

Don't bet on it, the father said.

Bed to wheelchair. Wheelchair to car. They rode, the daughter at the wheel, the father belted-in and looking straight ahead. He seemed not to be seeing the passing scenery, and unfamiliar with old neighborhoods, with what she named. There's that Dairy Queen, she said. Where you got the dented fender. And there's the park. It seems smaller, doesn't it? And look—the pond's gone, all dried up.

He shifted in his seat. Tearful, uneasy. He rolled down the window and watched road signs zip by. Tell me something, he said. Where are we?

You tell me, she said. What road are we on? What year is this? And while we're at it, who's the President.

Are you nuts? the father said.


She took the long way, a detour along a quiet street. Recognize this? she said, slowing down. Her childhood home, a house in the Tudor style: decorative timber, stucco, rough brick.

Sure, he said. Who wouldn't?

After all these years, I thought you'd like to see, she said.

The house, he said. Well. Look at that.

They looked.

Hasn't changed a bit, the father said.

Except the lawn, she said of the well-trimmed and weedless green. When we lived here it never looked so good.

Yard work—I hardly bothered, the father said. But crabgrass—that sure as hell came up.

And dandelions—don't forget, the daughter said. But see? They left the roses, after all these years.

I need to pee, the father said.

I doubt it, the daughter said. You just went, she said. It's just a feeling. Probably spasms, she said, easing away from the curb, moving on.

~

The place was unfancy, roadside. A pizza in neon flashed in the window. Handicapped parking was not to be had. Come on, she said. She positioned his feet to the asphalt, got him in a pivot, put his hands to holding the upper edge of the car door. On three, she said. He rocked forward on each count, eyes closed, as if such concentration would assist. Three, the daughter said emphatically, and he began to stand. But no— legs collapsed, fingers slipped.

I can't, he said.

You can, the daughter said. And seeing the daughter to be relentless he heaved himself forward. See? she said. He was standing, shaking, holding on. Now walk, she said.

And he came ahead, picking his feet up as he had been instructed to do, moving in a motion most unnatural, nearly mechanical. (Had he not politely told that busy-body therapist, that candy-assed woman, to get out or give it a rest?) Heavily on the daughter's arm he came, the distance not terribly far, the daughter pointed out.

I can't make it, the father said.

Sure you can, she said. (Christ. Did she not know when to quit?)

A small commotion ensued in the entranceway involving the logistics of simultaneously bracing the door, and supporting his weight. I've got you, she said.

Diners turned for a better look: an old man lumbering through the doorway held upright by a getting-older woman. Let me get that, someone said, holding the door.

The father swayed. Teetered.

Catch me, he told the daughter. A sweat had emerged. A pallor most cold. A chair was hurried under. I'm wet, he said, pulling at the seat of his pants but sitting anyway, sitting in it. What a mess, he said.

The daughter fetched slices on paper plates and sodas in paper cups. She positioned a slice in his hands. (Would she not cease and desist?)

Let's go, he said before even a bite. Let's go. No good.

Good for nothing, he said when she had him back home and hosed down, as she called it, and—in fresh pajamas—back in bed.

There, she said. All cleaned up and no harm done.

Says who? the father said.

But that hair, she said cheerily. Let me get to that.

Don't bother, he said.

No bother, she said, unzipping the tote and rummaging through for the comb and scissors.

Another time, he said.

Uneven strands. Sprigs. The daughter has come to tidy things up. Nearly all has recently been cut to a stubble, except for the places the lawn mower has missed. Bits of decorations have been blown about—the petal of an artificial rose, a ribbon shredded by the mower blades, a piece of someone's wreath. She notes seeds have been scattered and that new grass is growing everywhere, except inside this oblong plot. Here there are only weeds—crabgrass, dandelion, a tangle of thready stems. A general messiness. Well. She kneels and zips opens the satchel. It has never been unpacked.

The comb is there. And the little brush for dusting. The scissors, too. She trims back the stalks that bend to the lettered stone. (Could he know how overgrown it had become, how derelict?) She takes the brush and whisks away the snips of green that fall along granite edge.

# IN OTHER HEMISPHERES

The land slips by below him—towns and treetops, bridges and rivers. Upland fog. The glitter of water.

The father tries to see. Ground, he says. Low visibility. Ground, come in.

Shh, the daughter says.

Tower? the father says. Do you read me on this frequency?

You'd better hold it down, the daughter says.

Attempting to land. Trying to get home.

Listen, says the daughter. There is no plane. There's no going home.

No going home, the father says.

No, she says. Just look around.

The father looks. The surrounding space is vast but somehow close. Still the land passes under: farmland, deserts, old airfields of a former war.

Thin clouds. Wind sound. And this, too: the smell of cut wood, of pine, of places darkly forested. The father stretches out his hand: there the cradling boards.

Well? the daughter says.

Now I remember, the father says. For a minute I thought I was back in a cockpit.

Could confuse anyone, the daughter says.

The walls are so close and there was the sound of an engine.

Engine? says the daughter

Or maybe it was just the wind. But I saw the old runways. I saw the night sky.

But now you remember. Now you know where you are.

Sure, says the father. I've got it now.

Do you remember that I fixed your pillow? That I said goodnight?

What you said was: See you tomorrow.

I thought I would, the daughter says. I thought I'd have more time—that you would have more time.

The room was dark, the father says. Then darker. It happened so quickly, I couldn't call out. I thought I smelled grain—wheat or oats—what horses eat. A clean, sweet smell. There was a field and a gate. There were stars overhead, but I couldn't get my bearings. The stars seemed from some other hemisphere. Then I shit my pajamas. There was nothing I could do. I heard footsteps in the hall. Voices I didn't know. It seemed like hours before somebody noticed.

Noticed you were dead?

Noticed I was dead, noticed I shit my pajamas. Dead or alive, eventually you shit your pajamas.

They washed you after, says the daughter. According to custom. I made sure.

I remember the water. The cloth they used. The box. The lid.

It's pine, says the daughter. With a hand-rubbed finish.

It's something like the paneling we put up in the basement. Knotty pine they called it then.

The funeral guy—he was pushing the oak.

I'll bet he was.

More durable—the oak—that's what he said.

Goddamn crooks, every one of them. He was probably just over-stocked on oak. Probably had oak coming out his ass.

Could be, says the daughter.

They've got you by the nuts, these funeral guys. That should be their motto: In Your Time Of Need, We've Got You By The Nuts.

Well, I went with the pine, but I did splurge on the lining.

The lining's not bad. A decent lining.

I told him the lining better be decent. That you knew linings.

In the clothing business, you had to know.

I think it's polyester, the daughter says.

Could be poly, could be rayon. It's hard to tell exactly in this light.

There's light? You've got light?

There's some kind of light. Dim, though, like moonlight.

Too early for the moon, the daughter says.

Then it has to be something that runs on a battery. A night-light, or something.

I really doubt it, the daughter says. It's a Jewish coffin. They don't go in for coffin nightlights. I barely got you buried in your old flight jacket.

What's wrong with the jacket?

You know. That Jewish thing. When you go, you're supposed to be biodegradable.

No nails in the coffin, the father says. No hinges. No buttons.

And no zippers, says the daughter.

Still fits, says the father.

Check the pocket, says the daughter. Right hip.

That's where I used to keep my compass.

It's not a compass, says the daughter.

Hold on. Here's something. Well what have we got here?

Old photographs. Stuff I saved. I stuck them in at the very last minute.

Well, look at this. What do you know.

That's you, see? There you are. Beside a plane.

B-17, the father says.

And see? There. You're wearing your jacket.

Looked damn good on me back then.

Still does, says the daughter.

Might keep me warm yet, the father says.

Might, she says. That and the shroud.

Shroud? Oh sure. What's death without a shroud.

The funeral guy said you needed it. He said it was customary—a Jewish thing.

Another Jewish thing.

He said: Go with the oak and I'll throw in the shroud.

Pushing that oak, the father says. What a business. A license to steal.

I had a choice—linen or cotton. So I went with the cotton.

Always better. Less wrinkles than linen, says the father.

You always told me that cotton breathes.

Breathing, the father says. That's a good one. Too late now, wouldn't you say?

Not you, says the daughter. Not you—the cloth. Cotton, as opposed to something synthetic.

What's the thread count? Did he tell you?

I never asked, the daughter says.

You have to die nowadays to get a decent thread count. It should be alright.

A shroud and a flight jacket. All I need, I guess.

Check the other pocket. Left chest.

That's where I usually kept my flight plan.

It's just one more photograph, the daughter says.

Well look at this. Where was this taken?

See the sign? says the daughter. Happy Animal Sanctuary.

Well sure. Sure. I remember. It was sort of a zoo.

A big outdoor zoo with a fence all around, the daughter says.

There I am at the gate, the father says.

And there's me, says the daughter.

You must have been six, maybe seven.

I cried about the animals in cages. The bears and the wolf. I remember a poor old tiger.

But the deer were loose, the father says. They were loose and walking around right next to the people. We were all fenced in.

See? By the gate—there's a deer. A little buck.

I remember that deer, says the father. We got deer food from a little machine.

You put in a quarter and out came some grain.

I opened the gate to see if he'd go out, says the father.

You held the food out to him, in your hand. You tried to coax him through the gate.

But he wouldn't go. I remember that deer, the father says. He wouldn't go.


Shh, the daughter says. Someone's coming.

Who? says the father. Who would be coming?

It's the men who will carry you. Shh now, the daughter says.


All through, ma'am? asks one of the men.

With what? says the daughter.

With whatever you've been doing.

I'm not doing anything, the daughter says.

No rush though, says the other man. No rush at all.

We can wait if you think that you need more time.

No, the daughter says. No more time.


The men step in closer and put their hands on the box. Get that end, one says.

Got it, says the other.

What's going on? says the father. Where are we going?

You know, don't you? the daughter says.

Ready on three, the first man says. One, two, and OK, good.

Hey. Take it easy, the father says. Easy now.

A joggle, a tilt.

Watch it, the father says. Watch what you're doing.

The men step through a doorway. A little to your left, one man says.

We're moving, says the father.

They're bringing you along, says the daughter.

Hold on a minute, the father says. Where will you be? Where are you going?

I'll just be up front. You ride in the back.

Daughter? he says.

Me? she says. Did you mean me?

Yes—you. Of course—you. Who else would I mean? Who the hell else?


The long car is waiting. The rear doors are swung open: the carpeted interior, tinted windows, the oddness of curtains.

The box is pushed inside. The men shut the doors. The daughter wonders if the box will be secure on wide turns and sudden stops. There is not much weight. The father had become so thin, so narrow in the shoulder. So spindly in the leg.

The motor starts. Engine-hum, headlights.

We're moving, the father says. We're going faster now.

We're on the freeway.

Where, exactly?

Still in the world, the daughter says.

What does that mean? the father says.

There is still sky, still trees.

And clouds? the father says.

Oh sure, she says. Wonderful clouds.

Which? the father says.

Cirrus, mostly.

No, he says. Say it the way you say it. As if you're writing. The way you say it with that writing crap you write.

Sure, the daughter says. How about this: To the north are strays of cirrus, gold-spun with sunrise.

Very nice.

Thank you.

And to the south? the father says.

To the south—cumulonimbus in an indigo sky.

What to the west? the father says.

To the west I don't know, the daughter says.

Then make something up. You're good at that.

Alright, she says. How about some fields? How about some waves of grain, that sort of thing?

Fine, he says. I liked flying over fields.

To the west, says the daughter, is a thresher cutting its way through the waves of wheat. A golden dust rises above the blades.

Again with the gold, the father says.


A sense of space ensues. Shadows snap past: the criss-cross of steel, a suspension of cables.

I know we are somewhere high, the father says. I feel as if we are over water.

We are, says the daughter.

I've always felt it, the father says. On those long flights over the ocean, even in the dark. A pulling in your blood. Even a river or a stream would do it—the feeling of water passing beneath you. I feel it now.

We're on the bridge.

See? I knew it. Over the Hudson. Where are we headed?

Downtown, says the daughter.

Downtown? says the father. This time of day? You'd be better off taking the FDR Drive.

The Drive? says the daughter. I really don't think so. The West Side is better.

You're nuts, says the father. It's all stop and go; it's lights all the way from 59th on down.

Driver! calls the daughter. Can you hear me?

Lady? says the driver.

Stay left at the toll booth and take The Drive.

The driver looks back in his rear view mirror. The Drive, Lady? he says. You gotta be kidding. This time of day?

The long car pulls to the curb and stops.

Now what? says the father.

A little detour, says the daughter.

Where are we? The end of the line?

Not yet, the daughter says.

Then where? he says.

I told you, says the daughter. Way down town. East Houston and Ludlow.

Katz's? says the father. You bring a dead man downtown to Katz's.

Sure. Why not?

Here's why not: See that sign? No parking, no standing. It's a tow-away zone.

I think it's alright.

Plus the cops and their end-of-the-month parking blitz, the father says.

They won't tow if someone's in the car.

Good point, says the father. He calls to the driver: Hey driver. Yeah, you—up front.

The driver looks in his rearview mirror. Yo. What's up? the driver says.

We're stopping here. We shouldn't be too long.

Take your time, the driver says. He takes off his cap.

If a cop comes by, tell him it's a funeral.

You got it pal, the driver says.

And put on your flashers, the father says.

No problem, says the driver, coming around to the rear. Here, he says. Let me get those doors.

Who's next? calls the counterman.

Over here, says the father.

Whooo! Papi, says the counterman peering over the counter. You OK?

Sure, the father tells the counterman.

I think you be needing some big kind of sandwich.

Pastrami on rye, the father tells him. Heavy on the mustard.

Bueno, says the counterman. Coming right up. He opens the meat case. He hoists a great fat-crusted stump to the slicer. He leans it to the blade.

The counterman's tip cup is taped to the countertop. The father reaches up and puts in a bill.

Gracias, says the counterman.

Forget it, says the father.

Forget it nothing, the counterman says. Not everybody tip.

It's alright, the father says.

How you like, says the counterman. Thick or thin?

Nice and thin, the father says. And don't trim the fat.

The counterman adjusts the slicer. He flips the toggle switch. He slides the lever back and forth. How 'bout them Yankees? the counterman says.

Bums, says the father.

What to drink? says the counterman. We got seltzer, we got cream. Cel-Ray. Black cherry. Out of Pepsi.

Cream, says the father.

Ice or no, says the counterman.

No, says the father. It'll be cold enough.

To stay or go? the counterman says.

To stay, says the father. I wish to stay.

Papi, says the counterman.

~

City streets, traffic stops. Another bridge. The hollow hum of tires on the bridgeway grids.

How much further, the father says.

Not much, the daughter says. We got a little lost when we took that detour.

We should have a navigator.

No need, the daughter says.

Then who knows the way?

You do. You always did. You never got lost.

I'd feel a lot better if I had my compass, the father says. Or even a look at some familiar stars.

There'll be night I expect, the daughter says. Or some sort of night.

So stars at least, the father says.

The dipper, the bear. The flying horse.

Just listen to you, the father says.

Listen to me.

It all sounds so pretty, the father says.

It makes it easier, don't you think?

Don't you believe it, says the father.

I don't, the daughter says. I don't believe it. I never would.

They drive on. Neighborhoods are passing. Houses, fences, sidewalks, yards. A woman with flowers. A man with a beard. An old dog in a red coat.

Birds drop from the wires, one by one, then circle and meet in the air.

Are we stopping? the father says. It feels like we are.

Roadwork, says the daughter. Just relax.

Easy for you, the father says. You're not going where I'm going.

No, the daughter says. Not just yet.

The wipers come on.

Rain, says the father. I figured it would rain.

How did you know? the daughter says.

Cumulonimbus, says the father.

I forgot my umbrella, she says.

There might be a canvas for people to stand under.

Usually is, the daughter says.

There'll be water where they've been digging. At the bottom.

There's water in the gutter.

Tell me, says the father.

Things—small things—are riding down the gutter with the rain. A paper bag, a cigarette. A crust of bread someone has tossed away.

Who would do such a thing? the father says.

Now a lottery ticket is floating by. And a paper—a letter, I think—that someone has lost. There's a sparrow perched along the curb. There's a yellow leaf sliding down the grate.

To see it all again, the father says.

~

We're getting close, says the father.

Yes, we are. We're very near, the daughter says.

Time, distance, speed of travel. I know these things, the father says.

Are you ready? she says.

I'm not sure if I am. I'm not sure if I'm not.

Well, here we are. At the cemetery. Turning in now. Now we're going through the gate.

I remember the deer, the father says.

Daddy, the daughter says.

Angel, says the father.

Who? says the daughter. Do you mean me?

No, not you. Why the hell you?

Just asking, she says.

But there—there it is—I see one flying by.

That? That's a bird, says the daughter.

Not an angel.

I don't think so, says the daughter.

I didn't either—not really, says the father. All bullshit, he says.

Most things, says the daughter

And that place in the photograph—that place with the deer—that wasn't a sanctuary.

I guess not, the daughter says.

Even with the gate open, there was no place to go.

Here we are, the daughter says. We're here.

The long car stops. The doors are flung open. The men slide the box along the long car's bed. They lift the box onto the cart. The wheels flatten the wet grass and bump over the ruts.

Whoa, says the father. What's the rush? Tell these guys to slow down, will you?

Hey, says the daughter. You guys. Slow down.

Thank you, says the father. Thanks for everything.

Don't thank me, she says.

Why the hell not? he says.

I hate all of this.

I'll be alright, he says.

I don't know, says the daughter.

I don't either, says the father.

The men stop. The box is steadied. Rain falls on the polished wood.

Well, says the father. So much for the hand-rubbed finish.

The daughter laughs. Yes—she says—so much for that.

I smell the grass, the father says.

It's where they were digging, the daughter says. Where the sod was cut.

Get under the canvas so you don't get wet, the father says.

I am, says the daughter.

Can you hear me? says the father.

Daughter? he says. Are you there?


The father descends. The mounting hush and rumble of approaching weather engulfs him. He hears the downpour of small stones falling on the wood. Ground—he calls—Visibility poor.

He reaches into his jacket pockets for what he once carried: right hip for compass, left chest for flight plans. But they are not to be found. They will not be required. There will be no need for the instruments of navigation. There are metals in the earth.

Ground—the father calls again—We have westerly cross-winds; we have steady precipitation. Must divert. Must divert.

The land that sped below him now comes up to meet him. Here are the dark rows of the fields in tillage. Here is the mud of roadside ditches, the dust of desert basins.

The soil rains down—now a fistful in the daughter's hand. Now the shovelful of loam.

# ACKNOWLEDGMENTS

With gratitude to George Rand, the literary journal editors who published the stories, and the staff at Fiction Collective Two and the University of Alabama Press.

Stories and excerpts from *Paradise Field* previously appeared in the following literary journals: "Jerusalem" in *Black Warrior Review*; "As Those Who Know the Dead Will Do" in *NY Tyrant*; "Somewhere in the North Atlantic" and "Recognizable Constellations and Familiar Objects of the Night Sky in Early Spring" in *Parcel*; "There's Nothing Here You'd Want" in *Gulf Coast*; "Paradise Field," "Inscription," "Details of Grief," "The Rhythm of Digging," "In This Last Slipping-Past Year," and "The Song Inside the Plate" in *Unsaid*; "Arrow Canyon" and "The Renoir Is Put Straight" in *The Brooklyn Rail*; "In Other Hemispheres" in *Bellevue Literary Review*; and "Mitzvah" in *JewishFiction.net*.

An excerpt from "Interment for Yard & Garden: A Practical Guide" appeared in *The Ilanot Review* and in its entirety in *The Brooklyn Rail*.